If there's one thing I'm good at it's coping. It's what I do.

Suddenly Milly finds that she *can't* cope, after all, with her mother's unhappiness, her father's desertion, and her own anger. She runs away to her gran, who has always been a refuge in times of trouble. But this time it is Gran who needs help, to recall the faces from her childhood which are beginning to fade from her memory. To escape from her own problems, Milly decides to help Gran chase the faces from her past—and in doing so finds the strength to face up to her own future, whatever it holds.

Pam Scobie was born in Birmingham and studied English at Cambridge. She taught for a number of years then retrained as an actress at the Webber-Douglas Academy in London. While working with a Theatre-in-Education team in Wales, she began writing for the company. Her first novel *A Twist of Fate* was based on one of her early plays. Her second *The School That Went On Strike* was short-listed for the Whitbread Children's Novel Award. *Chasing Faces* is her fifth novel for Oxford University Press.

Chasing Faces

Other books by Pamela Scobie

A Twist of Fate
The School That Went On Strike
Stand Up Now
Children of the Wheel

Chasing Faces

Pamela Scobie

OXFORD
UNIVERSITY PRESS

OXFORD
UNIVERSITY PRESS

Great Clarendon Street, Oxford OX2 6DP

Oxford University Press is a department of the University of Oxford.
It furthers the University's objective of excellence in research, scholarship,
and education by publishing worldwide in

Oxford New York

Athens Auckland Bangkok Bogotá Buenos Aires Calcutta
Cape Town Chennai Dar es Salaam Delhi Florence Hong Kong Istanbul
Karachi Kuala Lumpur Madrid Melbourne Mexico City Mumbai
Nairobi Paris São Paulo Shanghai Singapore Taipei Tokyo Toronto Warsaw
and associated companies in Berlin Ibadan

Oxford is a registered trade mark of Oxford University Press
in the UK and in certain other countries

British Library Cataloguing in Publication Data available

ISBN 0 19 271849 5

1 3 5 7 9 10 8 6 4 2

Typeset by AFS Image Setters Ltd, Glasgow

Printed and bound in Great Britain by
Biddles Ltd, Guildford and King's Lynn

For my mother

I should like to thank Ron, Kathy, and Kate for getting and keeping me on the right track, for their patience, clear-sightedness, and generosity.
And my mother, who always made everything possible.

1

She walked in and caught me.

'Where d'you think *you*'re going?' she screeched, right in my face. She thinks that's the way to break my cool—poor deluded creature.

'Don't tell me you *care*.' I carried on dropping T-shirts, perfectly ironed and folded (by me, naturally), into the suitcase on the bed.

'I *don't* care! I'm the worst mother in the world! I have to know in case you commit a felony!' She watches too many American cop dramas, but there's no telling her.

'I'm going to Gran's. Any objections?'

She shut up at that. A miracle. But only a short one.

'You breathe *one* word to her about this, and—'

'Do me a favour. We'll have better things to talk about.'

'Like *what*?' She shrieked with artificial laughter. 'Your project for the summer hols? Be my guest!' I ducked, as my ancient ring-binder came flapping towards me and crashed into the wall with a squawk.

'Nice one, Mum. But I've already packed the laptop. Call me when you feel ready for an adult conversation.'

I walked downstairs and out of the front door, counting under my breath the number of seconds before the inevitable cave-in.

Ten, eleven, twelve . . .

The bedroom window flew up.

'Don't forget your pencil-case!' It burst on the gravel by my foot. The window slammed.

Well, well. Even mothers can surprise you sometimes.

2

'Are you *sure* you've told me everything about this weekend, Milly? You're not hiding anything from me?'

'Sorry, Gran. This is as interesting as it gets. Dad's in Brussels pitching for the Snappy Nappy account, and Mum's belly-dancing in Llandudno. So you're stuck with me till Monday, I'm afraid.'

I'm good at this. Lying through my teeth. It's a wonder they don't all jump out of my mouth in protest. Mind you, all that stuff was true. It just hadn't happened *this* weekend.

'Belly-dancing! Joanna should have cancelled.'

'It wasn't her turn.' It always feels so *weird* when Gran calls Mum by her name, as if she's somebody completely different, a stranger, almost. 'But you know Dad. Work comes first.' I'd said it again. *Dad*. A syllable made out of Semtex. Still—not so different from *dead*. If I remembered that every time I had to use it, it would get easier and easier.

I took a mouthful of coffee, and missed.

'*Oh, SHH—!*'

'Shut your lips and shout sugar!' laughed Gran, tossing me a cloth.

'*What?*' I scrubbed at the front of my blouse. It was going to mark, I just knew it. Unbearable, unendurable, and on top of everything else—

'Shut your lips and shout sugar! It's what my mother always used to say whenever there was something horrid

2

to put up with, like having nothing but cold water to soothe our itches when we had chickenpox. You're not usually clumsy.'

'It's my age. Adolescent poltergeists . . . I've only got to walk into a room and precious family ornaments start hurling themselves off the sideboard like lemmings.'

'You're overtired, that's all. Get yourself into bed, and I'll come and tuck you in in five minutes.'

Now let's get this straight. I don't get tucked in at home. I'm nearly sixteen, for crying out loud. But grans are different. You've got to humour them. Rise above it, know what I mean?

I went into the bathroom and locked the door. I changed into my pyjamas. All in all, it wasn't going too badly. I turned on the cold tap and got my tooth stuff out of my sponge bag. I squeezed three centimetres of paste on to the brush. I bared my smile at the mirror. I began to scrub, up, down, up,down.

Grief walked up behind me and punched me in the back. I jackknifed over the basin as tears came torrenting out of my eyes and nose. Froth spilled from my mouth, fizzing warm on my fingers, and was snatched and swirled away by the twisting water.

'Milly? *Milly?* Are you all right in there?'

I emptied my mouth. I grabbed a towel and blew my nose into it. In the mirror over the sink, my face was bright red, daubed with absurd smears of peppermint green.

'Fine, Gran! Just gargling!'

She was waiting for me when I came out.

'What's wrong? Did you think the U-Bend Monster had got me? The Thing that Comes up from the Plughole and Licks your Eyeballs Out?'

'My Auntie Franny used to lock herself in the bathroom,' said Gran. 'Mother said she was praying.' I followed her into the spare room and got into bed. 'You haven't got any daft ideas about being too fat, have you, Milly?'

It took me a second or two to catch on.

'I wasn't throwing up! I can't even watch people being sick on telly.'

'I hate that too.' Gran shuddered. 'It seems to be obligatory nowadays, anything to shock.' She kissed my cheek, and I got a lovely whiff of her scent. Amazing what happens to the cheapest yuck (even re-cycled *Christmas* yuck), as soon as Gran dabs it on. If you could market the chemical reaction, you'd make squillions. 'Are you *sure* you're all right, Milly? You've never talked about the divorce. How it's affected you.'

'Because it hasn't. All frightfully civilized. Everybody still bestest of friends.'

She sighed. 'Your mother never tells me anything either.'

'Well, *that's* because there's nothing left to tell after it's been through her grief counsellor, her women's group, Brenda next door, the dog, the cat, the budgie, and everybody she was ever at school or Guide camp with. I'm *joking*, Gran.' I wasn't. 'We haven't got a budgie.'

'Anybody but me.' Gran looked sad. 'That's *my* fault, I suppose, along with everything else. But our generation didn't go in for all this soul-baring. You and me are two of a kind, Milly. We keep it all inside. We shut our lips and shout sugar.'

'I'm not shouting anything,' I said.

'And Auntie Franny wasn't praying.'

We looked at each other.

''Nighty-'night, then, pet.' She went out, humming to herself. You can always hear where Gran is, even if you can never quite make out the tune . . .

4

I was a bit narked that she thought I'd been making myself sick. I mean. Eating disorders are for people who can't cope, aren't they? And if there's one thing I'm good at it's coping. It's what I do.

I shut my eyes, and it all came whirling round again, as if it was trapped on some horrible loop. There was Mum, flicking spaghetti at the wall (we meant to stop doing that after we decorated, but it's the only way to see if it's cooked), making little digs at Dad, the kind he doesn't *really* mind. And there's Sherrylynne, tittering and twittering, like she always does, trying to pretend she belongs, which she doesn't and she never can do, no matter what Dad—

And . . . *cut*! No way was I going through *that* again.

I got out of bed and headed for the bookcase. I needed to open a trapdoor and dive down a flight of pages into somewhere else. Ah! *Wuthering Heights*. Just the job! I hooked my finger into the top of the spine and tugged, and something that had been squeezed in between it and the next book along dropped out on to the rug. It was a little package wrapped in a sheet of A4.

If I told you it spoke to me and said, *Open me! Open me!* you wouldn't believe it, would you? Well, it did. Sort of. I mean, Gran *never* does stuff like that. She has a place for everything. This was like it had been hidden in a hurry. Or forgotten. Or lost. And hey—just what kind of secrets is an old-age pensioner going to have anyway?

Inside the packet were a lot of bits of old torn-up photograph, the browny-coloured sort that's seriously ancient. And the paper it was wrapped in had writing on. Gran's, by the look of it.

I wasn't sure what to do first. Piece the picture together or read the writing? I'm better with words than pictures, so I went for the writing. What's that? You'd have done it

5

the other way? You wouldn't have done it at all? Oh, come on! You're *just* as nosy as I am.

Well, go on. Take a look. See if *you* can make any sense out of it . . .

3

On a clean May morning in nineteen-twenty-six, Jack Whately put on his cap, tied his muffler round his throat, kissed his wife on the cheek, and got ready to walk out of the house just like any ordinary man.

'Oh, Jack—be careful,' begged his wife.

'You're a fool,' said Beryl, his eldest, who was able to get away with things. 'I'll walk you to the top of the road.'

'Can I come?' pleaded Emmy.

'You're too little,' said Jack Whately. 'You stay here and look after your mother. And the Son and Heir. You keep them out of trouble.'

Beryl took his arm. She was his Special Girl.

'Off we go, then.'

By noon, everybody in the street knew what he'd been up to. But it wasn't until nightfall and chucking-out time that the trouble started . . .

*   *   *

'*I'll* take that, if you don't mind. Thank you.' Gran pushed the bits of torn-up photo into the pocket of her dressing-gown. 'And the rest.'

I put the crumpled paper into her outstretched hand.

'I'm sorry, Gran.' She didn't look *too* mad, thankfully. 'Is it a book? Are you writing a book?' Hey, that would be *cool*. My Gran, the novelist!

She shook her head.

'It's of no interest to anybody else. Just things that happened when I was a little girl in the Depression.'

'But we're doing that next term! Gran, that's brilliant!'

'And your mother never mentioned—?'

'Oh, she's useless! *She* said the Slump is what happens when I sit down in front of the telly. So *I* said she should donate her sense of humour to science, then they can pinpoint the wonky gene and zap it out, and anyway *I* always thought the Depression was what happened the weekend she ran out of Prozac.'

'How long's she been on Prozac?'

'It's just an expression,' I said hastily. 'Hey—are *you* in it? Which one are you? Beryl? No—Emmy!'

'Yes, well, it's time you were asleep. Back into bed now, quick. Good lass.' She straightened the covers and stood, looking down at me for a moment. 'I'll tell you one thing, though. It's a fallacy that hard work never killed anybody. Because it does.' She turned off the lamp.

'Don't go.' I wanted to be pampered, indulged. Not to be left alone. 'Tell me what happened after the pubs shut.'

I felt her hesitate.

'Promise to tell something in return?'

'Sure.' I could always lie.

She switched on the lamp again, and sat down beside me in the small circle of light that the darkness, like a cupped hand, held motionless.

'Close your eyes then,' she said.

I closed my eyes . . .

*   *   *

'What's that noise?' whispered the little girl.

'Nothing, dear. Close your eyes now, and go to sleep.'

'It's *not* nothing! *Listen!* Can't you hear it?'

8

'Only some men in the street. Close your eyes now, and think nice thoughts and it'll soon be morning.'

'But I don't know what to think about,' whimpered the child. 'And there are bad things inside my eyes.'

'Think about Christmas trees.' Her mother's hand, small and dry and smelling of bleach, reached down, closing Emmy's eyes for her, stroking her cheek. 'Sparkling and green and lovely. A whole forestful. Can you see them? Sparkling and lovely . . . ' The hand drifted away . . .

'I *can't* see them, you're going too fast.' Emmy clutched at the darkness, and it slid through her fingers like black sand.

'That's enough, Emmy.' There was an edge to the voice now. 'You're nearly seven, too old for this nonsense.'

'But the noise—'

'There's no noise. Just a bit of summer thunder. Keep those eyes shut, no cheating. I'm going away now.'

Emmy felt the sweet face draw near to her own. A strand of warm hair tickled her nose. She sucked in the warmth and the sweetness as if she could somehow breathe in her mother's spirit with them and hold it safe inside her. The soft mouth pressed a kiss at the side of her eye. The warmth retreated. She heard the hem of her mother's old serge skirt husking over the rug. Smelled her scent like a ghost fading.

'Don't go!' she cried wordlessly out of the blind and beating darkness. 'Don't go!' She opened her eyes and the tears ran stinging into her hair. 'Don't go,' she whispered into the worse than darkness. The door closed.

The sound was coming nearer. A sound like the steady crunching of blood that you get in your head sometimes when you lie on your ear the wrong way and squash it. But it wasn't inside her head. In the cramped front parlour on the other side of the wall, surely Mother and Beryl must hear it too. Crump! Crump! Crump! The sound of many boots champing the pavement, like the beating of a great, angry heart. Don't let it stop beating on our doorstep, prayed the little girl. Make it pass by.

The leading pair of boots stopped. Ker-clump! Then the pair behind. And the pair behind that. Ker-clump! Ker-*clump*! There was a graduated shuffling as the rest of the boots caught up. Then a moment of utter silence. But the heartbeat went on, a steady pulse of determination throbbing in the air.

Sounds from within the house. The clink of the fire-irons (somebody lifting the poker from its bracket in the front room). Whispers . . .

The door knocker went. Two loud claps. Emmy shrank down under her blanket in her bed in the alcove. She won't let them in, will she? Not so many of them? She won't let them in?

A squeaking sound. Somebody was pushing open the letter box. A voice bellowed through it:

'Come on out, man! Take what's coming to you!'

The door from the parlour opened, and Emmy heard her mother's light, uneven tread in the hall.

'Mother—*don't*!' shrieked Beryl.

'Go on home,' Elizabeth Whately told the letter box. 'Be sensible now. Go home.'

'What's this?' jeered the voice. 'Hiding behind your wife's skirts? Come on out, man, for shame!'

'My husband's no coward. It took a braver man than you are to do what he did today.'

'Look, missus, we've no quarrel with you—'

'That's not how it looks from here!'

'Will you just send him out?' The man's voice had lost energy. It sounded embarrassed and squashed from trying to post its opinions through the letter box. 'He knows how things are.'

'We all know how things are! Oh, it's fine for you union men, you look after each other. What's my man to do? Starve?'

'He should have stayed home today.'

'It's not his fight!'

'Well, it should be!' There were angry mutters from the rest of the men. Things weren't going the way they had expected. 'Will you send him out?'

'My children are every bit as hungry as yours.' Elizabeth Whately stood her ground. 'Why don't you go bullying the soldiers or the university boys? They did it for the fun of it! You think you're such big men, frightening women and bairns—'

'That's enough!' This was a new voice, harsh with impatience. No crouching by letter boxes for this one. 'Send him out now, this minute, or we'll come in and get him!'

'Just you try it!' Emmy couldn't believe this was her tiny mother talking. She sounded ready to take on the whole town.

There came a violent pounding on the front door, and the house rattled like a box of broken biscuits. Emmy shot out of bed and snatched Gus up out of his cot. He clung to her, yelling with fright. There were people in the alley as well now, kicking and hammering at the yard gate. As Emmy gazed in terror at the moon-thinned curtain, the moon came splashing through the glass, punched the curtain, and dropped with a thud on the floor.

The door burst open.

'What's happ—?' Beryl stepped into the room and moonlight crunched under her shoe.

'Don't move!' Elizabeth Whately ran briskly over the crackling floor and caught both children in her arms. Beryl struggled with the gas mantle. There was a hiss! and a plop! and the walls were stained with a thin, yellow light,

11

through which the ancient roses on the wallpaper shimmered faintly. 'Dear God!' mouthed Elizabeth Whately, her eye on the empty cot. It was full of shivers of broken moon. And all around them, the threadbare carpet was strewn with moonsplinters, diamond bright, diamond deadly.

Abruptly, the pounding stopped.

They stared at each other.

'What's it mean?' whispered Beryl. The men were holding themselves still, listening for something. There came two whistle blasts, and all the feet started shuffling at once. 'It's the police!' cried Beryl. There was a third blast, and the retreating feet speeded up, scattering. A pair of boots studded with authority came ringing over the pavement and the letter box flapped open again.

'Everything all right in there?'

'Yes, officer!' Beryl was overcome by giggles of relief. 'Will I let him in, Mother?'

'You will not!' Elizabeth Whately hastened into the hall. 'It's all right, officer,' they heard her telling the letter box. 'There's no harm done.'

'Aye, well.' The letter box sounded disappointed. 'Happen I'll just walk up and down for a bit, in case any of them takes it into his head to come back.'

'Just as you like, officer. Goodnight.' Elizabeth Whately limped back into the room. Pursing her lips, she stooped and picked up the moon from out of a puddle of splinters. All the moonlight had gone out of it. It looked just like a brick. The clouds parted above the back yard, and the real moon was back in its place, shining fiercely behind the curtain.

'Why didn't you tell them he wasn't here?' asked Emmy. 'They'd have gone away then.'

'Ssshh!' Elizabeth Whately pressed the tip of a finger to Emmy's lips. On the still night air, they heard the sound of a distant train disappearing. 'It's all right now,' she breathed. 'It doesn't matter who knows now.'

'Will they come back?'

'No,' said Beryl. 'But we'll sit up anyway.' Beryl was fifteen and took her responsibilities seriously.

But Emmy had not lain long awake before she felt her sister creeping into bed beside her. Elizabeth Whately watched all night, her arms tightly wound around Gus, the Son and Heir, who was still just small enough to fit into her lap.

Gus slept deeper than a drowned thing, his thumb in his mouth, his body curled against his mother's, as if they were still one shape, one being, the same blood beating through both hearts.

Pressed up against Beryl's bony hip, Emmy dreamed of a lost and lovely time when *she* had been allowed to sleep with Mother when Father was away. No time was ever safer or sweeter. Unutterable peace and stillness. Everything still to come. Nothing a threat. Like waiting to be born.

I wish, I wish, she thought—and stopped herself just in time.

They say you should be careful what you wish for.

You might just get it.

4

And what did she mean by *that*?
I was awake. Amazing. I hadn't expected to
sleep ever again.

'Breakfast's ready!'

I was actually hungry. Even more amazing. I'd been
quite sure I'd never be able to do anything as normal as
eating toast. It would have seemed a hollow mockery. But
it was surprisingly easy. Especially when somebody else
had made it.

'D'you want to give your mother a ring?' asked
Gran.

'Not allowed,' I said quickly. 'Female bonding stuff,
you know.' I bit off a huge mouthful and chewed pointedly
so she couldn't ask any more questions, then I took a big
swig of tea and switched the subject. 'So, why was there a
lynch mob outside your house?'

'Ever heard of the General Strike?'

'Erm . . . nineteen-twenty-something? That's what you
said last night.'

'That's it! They wanted to cut the miners' wages, can
you believe such wickedness? They only got about a pound
a week as it was—that's less than a hundred now—and
there was no Income Support. All the heavy industries
came out in sympathy.'

'So your dad was a blackleg?'

'He was not! He wasn't in a union, I *told* you that.
And we were flat broke, it was a terrible time for everyone.
They offered him a couple of days' work on the railways.

14

Somebody spotted him and he had to leave town fast. We never saw a penny of the money.'

'Was he right or wrong?'

'He put his family first. Right or wrong?'

'Makes a nice change . . . '

'Sorry?'

'Nothing! So what happened next day?'

'Beryl went looking for work. Well, what else could she do? The shops weren't on strike, and she'd her eye on a job selling radios . . . '

*   *   *

'And if I don't go, they'll only get somebody else,' said Beryl, peeling her stockings off the back of the chair.

'Are those dry?' asked her mother.

'Near enough.' Beryl sat down. 'They can dry on me.' She drew a slim, bare knee up to her nose, crunched one of the stockings into a shape like a little pocket and wiggled her toes into it.

'You'll catch a cold in your kidneys.'

'And if I sit too near the fire, I'll melt the marrow in my bones. And if I eat my crusts up, my hair will curl.'

'And you'll be no use to anyone if you're ill.'

Beryl shrugged, and straightened her leg, smoothing the stocking all the way up. She had wonderful legs, had Beryl, long and slim. Boys whistled and hooted when she went past, and grown men fell off ladders. Beryl didn't mind a bit. Emmy had an idea she minded more when they didn't.

'And stop admiring yourself!' snapped Elizabeth Whately. 'Everybody's got legs.'

Beryl pulled a face, and drew on the second stocking with exaggerated care. She rolled both of them down to just below the knee, and secured them with the elastic garters which left two little dadoes of pink teethmarks in the flesh when she took them off at night.

'Don't look like that, Mother. It's the fashion.'

'Well, I'll never get used to it,' said Elizabeth Whately. 'Showing your legs in the street. No wonder so many young girls nowadays come unstuck.'

'You've got to keep up with the times. If I get this job, I'm going to get me some real *silk* stockings. I'm sick of rotten old cotton.' Beryl stood up, shaking her dress straight. Sideways on, she looked as if she had no chest at all, but Emmy knew that, underneath her cami, Beryl's embarrassing bosoms were bound flat with an elastic bandage, so that her dress would hang the way it was meant to, straight up and down. There was a word for girls like Beryl, who bobbed their hair and their skirts (Beryl did both on the same day with the same pair of scissors). Flappers, that's what they called them.

She pulled on her hat that was shaped like the bell of a flower, and tugged it down round her face so that her chin looked tiny and her eyes enormous.

'Wish me luck!' she said. And out she went.

Elizabeth Whately sank down on the bed.

'Give us a kiss, Emmy.' She tapped her cheek. 'Just here. I need one.' Emmy clambered up beside her, and kissed the precious place that would have been worn smooth from kissing, if kissing could have done the job, and stopped wishing that she was fifteen and dark and dashing instead of not quite seven and not quite blonde and not much of anything in particular. 'You don't mind staying off school again, do you, Em? You can look after Gus.'

'No,' whispered Emmy into her mother's soft, unbound bosom. 'I don't mind.'

She slid down from the bed, tugged on her boots and did up the laces. She got into her pinafore and pulled the rags out of her hair. Even in times of direst peril, Elizabeth

16

Whately put Emmy's hair in for her at night, and wound up her own on hideous metal pins—a good reason for not answering the door after nine, even to a policeman.

Gus wanted the privy.

'All right, but don't draw attention to yourselves.'

Mrs Wilcocks Next Door had just finished stringing her washing across the alley. Emmy heard her gate go. She knew that Mrs Wilcocks would be wearing her usual fierce expression and her apron with a row of pegs stuck round the top. She had every right to be fierce, with an angry husband and three angry sons all lurking indoors because of the strike.

A window flew up high in one of the house backs.

'It's all over!' a man shouted down. 'And we've *lost*. Thanks to *some folk* too stuck up to stand by their own!'

Emmy shooed Gus back into the kitchen.

'You'll have to use the chamber-pot,' she told him.

'Emmy! Will you watch that kettle for us?'

'Yes, Mother!' Emmy dragged a chair up to the shallow stone sink and climbed on to it. The milk jug was sitting in a couple of inches of cold water. She sniffed it. A bit sour, but not too bad. On the black iron stove, the old enamel kettle was starting to rattle its lid.

I suppose we'll be moving again, she thought, as she waited for it to boil.

They never lived anywhere long.

Not since the day, not yet far enough behind them, when Emmy had sat with her mother at the back of a steep, dark room, while her father was asked questions by a man in a tall chair. And Mother had got up, and cried out as if she were hurt, and sat down again, covering her eyes with her hand . . .

That day had a word to go with it. Bankrupt.

'We're not the only ones,' said Beryl. 'It's near impossible to make a go of anything the way things are.'

17

Since then, it had been one place after another. They'd even lived in the woods once with a lot of other homeless families in a row of shacks put up for soldiers coming back from the Great War. The authorities were ashamed of them, Elizabeth Whately reckoned, so they kept them out of sight. They had one room between them. It had a wood-burning stove in the middle with two hotplates for boiling things on and a pipe leading out through the roof. They lived on skimmed milk, and turnips, and salted oatmeal, and the wizened little potatoes the pickers left behind. Even here, Mother did her best to make a home for them out of the bits the judge had let her keep, her blankets and baking tins, and her old feather boa that she wore every day. She was wearing it when she stepped on an adder and her foot blew up like a bolster, so for a while she had two bad legs instead of just one and couldn't go out at all . . .

And now they were in Newcastle. Rude, rowdy city, clanging and clanking, with its steam hammers thunking and its sirens whooping, and its great, grey ships hooting at each other like big, ugly birds. And its streets full of angry men.

'Kettle's boiled,' said Emmy.

Elizabeth Whately was lying down. She had taken out the ugly metal pins, and her hair, half-brushed, was fanned out around her face, making it very small and pale. A mermaid, that's what she looked like in the gloom, with her long skirt hiding her poor legs, a mermaid washed up on a rock, stranded and dying for want of the sea . . .

'Is it turned off? Good lass.' She struggled up into a sitting position. Out of the combings from her hairbrush she had made herself a fake bun, around which she began lifting and winding her heavy tresses. The finished product would be like a great, chestnut-coloured cottage loaf, newly baked. But this morning, she looked so frail that the loaf seemed in danger of crushing her.

'Shall I start the packing?' asked Emmy.

'Oh, Em.' Elizabeth Whately gazed up at her with sad eyes. 'One day we'll have a big house again, I promise. You'll have your own room and your own bed, and everybody in town will know our name.'

'They know it now,' said Emmy.

'But one day it'll be because we're Somebody.'

After breakfast, Elizabeth Whately cleaned the carpet by strewing it with the three-days-old tea-leaves and scrubbing them off with the yard broom.

'We'll leave this place better than we found it. If we've got nothing else, we've got our self-respect.'

Emmy wrapped up some of her mother's precious bits in old newspaper and stowed them away in the battered hamper, ready for when Father's letter came, telling them where to join him.

The days went by and no letter came.

And then it was June, and Emmy's birthday.

'By rights you should have been born in May,' lamented Elizabeth Whately, as she did every year, 'but I held on. May's an unlucky month to be born in, and I should know. Fetch my purse, would you, Em?' She was lying down again. She'd been lying down a lot in the last few days.

'I'll bring you something tonight,' promised Beryl, rushing out of the house.

Emmy lugged over the big leather bag that was flat-bottomed from being dumped on the floor next to Mother's chair. She undid the clasp and breathed in the familiar smells of lavender and old face powder.

'Here's your purse.'

Elizabeth Whately looked inside it.

'Well now! Here's a whole sixpence!'

'Is it your lucky sixpence?' Elizabeth Whately had kept the same sixpence in her purse since the day she was married.

'And what if it is?'

'Then you've to keep it. You know what you say. So long as I've a sixpence in my purse, I know I'm not des—des—?'

'Destitute?' Her mother smiled wanly. 'So we're not quite destitute yet.' Her fingers drifted up to the deep crease between her eyebrows, that seemed to get deeper every day, and chafed the place as if trying to rub it smooth. Her face brightened. 'Why, look! Here's a ha'penny! It was hiding there all the time! This afternoon, you can run out and buy yourself an iced bun!'

*   *   *

'An iced bun!' I did a quick scroll through what I got for my last birthday. Mountain bike, trainers, CDs, a cheque. *And* they took me out for a meal, *and* they let me drink wine. The perfect family. We must have fooled the whole restaurant. Just thinking about it made me want to get all the presents in a pile and torch the lot.

'It was a big treat for a seven year old,' said Gran.

'And I suppose you can remember to this day exactly how it tasted?' I mocked.

Gran shook her head.

'It was the worst birthday of my life,' she said.

20

5

She stopped for a drink of water out of the horse trough to quell her hunger, and that's what made her late. If she hadn't been late, she could surely have stopped it happening.

She ran down the street, clutching the paper bag with the bun in it. There were people outside their front door. Beryl and Gus and Mrs Wilcocks and Her From Upstairs.

'Where've you *been*?' Beryl screamed at her.

'What's happened? Where's my mother?'

'They've took her away in the ambulance.' Mrs Wilcocks was scowling. Mrs Wilcocks only had the one expression. She wore it for everything: funerals, dealing with tradesmen, and whenever she was embarrassed by a kind instinct. 'I've give your little brother his tea.'

'There was no need,' said Beryl.

'She fell down in the yard,' said Her From Upstairs. 'They've took her away to make her better.'

'We'll manage by ourselves now, ta very much.' Beryl pushed open the front door. Emmy darted inside.

'Mother!' She ran into the front room, then into the back. '*Mother!*' In the kitchen, lost, she stood, waiting for the swish of the skirt, the brisk, irregular footsteps, the tight, comforting arms. Panicking, she ran out into the yard. '*Mother! Mother!*'

'Stop it!' Beryl grabbed at her. Emmy ducked under her arm and ran back inside, to the front room again, to the big, dark cupboard in the corner that looked so much like an upright coffin.

21

'Mother?' she whimpered, opening the door.

Her parents' clothes hung in front of her, like empty people, waiting for souls to inhabit them. She plucked at the arm of her father's old dress coat, as if to attract its attention. It was cold and stiff, smelling of long dead cigars and the cream he flattened his hair with. His ties were looped over a wire on the inside of the door and his spats folded in a corner with his cane propped up next to them. Even when his braces were frayed, and his shirt cuffs had to be shaved and his hair flattened with lard, Jack Whately walked the streets with a straight back, swinging that silver-topped cane. The Toff. That's what folk called him.

Her mother's dresses hung like wraiths, with necklaces of mothballs strung about the gaunt necks of the hangers. Emmy crept in among them and pulled the doors shut, squashing shoes beneath her as she hid herself in the folds of Mother's favourite dress, a grey, gauzy thing half covered with tiny, ice cold beads that were forever falling off, the one dress left from the Good Times, that Father would never let her sell. Crouched in the bottom of the wardrobe, she pressed the scratchy fabric against her face and shivered like an animal.

The door opened.

'Come on,' said Beryl gently. 'I've made us an egg.'

She had set two places. There was a plate and a spoon and a napkin each, and a boiled egg in a blue and white cup and one half each of Emmy's bun.

'Sit down, then.' Beryl lifted Gus on to her knee. She unfolded his napkin and tucked it into his front. To look at him, nobody would have guessed he was nearly four, he was that stunted from making do.

Emmy could see how much trouble Beryl had gone to to make it all nice, but it wasn't nice, any of it, it wasn't, and she couldn't bear it.

'Why's there only two eggs?'

'I don't want one.' Beryl sliced the top off Gus's egg and fed him a spoonful. 'Well, come on, Birthday Girl!'

Emmy was hurting all over with hunger, but she was too angry to eat.

'Why isn't there ever enough for all of us?' she raged. 'Why can't they look after us properly?'

'That's not fair.' Beryl dipped the spoon, and waved it in front of Emmy's mouth. Emmy turned her face away.

'When's she coming back?'

'When they've made her well.'

'When'll that be?'

'Soon. Meantime, you and Gus can stay with Auntie Beattie. You'll *love* it, Em. She's got a great big house with its own bathroom!' (Emmy was used to a tin basin on a board over the sink.) 'And Auntie Beattie *always* has enough to eat. Fresh bread and fresh milk and new laid eggs. Duck eggs,' Beryl added enticingly. 'Sky-blue duck eggs.'

Emmy stared bleakly at the humble hen's egg going cold on the table in front of her. She couldn't have cared less if it had been laid by a crocodile.

'She'll come and get you. The train comes all the way from her house to here.'

'But when will Moth—?' Emmy gulped, her mouth full of cold yellow yolk, about as appetizing as earwax. She shut her teeth, so she wouldn't get caught a second time.

'Honest, Em, it'll be just like a holiday.'

*   *   *

'Is that the time?' cried Gran. 'Why didn't you say? I've got to get to the supermarket, I've nothing for you to eat! Be an angel, Milly, and hold the fort. I'm expecting a parcel from my catalogue.'

The minute she drove off, the phone rang. I checked

my watch. Ten past ten! She'd held out longer than I'd expected.

It rang again at half past.

And again at a quarter to.

By eleven, I was ready to be magnanimous.

It didn't ring after that.

'Hasn't it come?' asked Gran, as I helped her unload the car. 'Isn't that *typical?*' She went indoors to call the company, and came back fuming. 'Can you believe it? They said they rang three times to check the address! I told them there was somebody here the whole time, but they wouldn't have it!'

She started asking little probing questions while we were making lunch. Like: 'Seen anything of Sherry-thing? What's her name? Your father's friend?'

'You mean his *partner?*' How I *loathe* that word. It sounds like they do a circus act together or something. I tried picturing Dad in tights and spangles, hanging off a trapeze by his teeth. But he hasn't the figure for it. A clown. That's more like it. A pathetic, sad old clown. Only he doesn't know it yet.

'Of course she's very young . . . but it's been a few months now, hasn't it? Are you still treating her as if she's invisible?'

'She won't last.'

'Milly, we have to face facts—'

No, we *don't*. I had to shut her up, I couldn't bear it. Not after last night. That smug little announcement. That big, ugly diamond on that horrible, nail-bitten finger . . .

I reverted to my stratagem for keeping Gran off the scent. A sort of *Arabian Nights* in reverse. If I could just keep her focused on Emmy and Gus, she wouldn't have time to chop my head off and view the horrors inside. Clever, huh?

24

'It's the *perfect* thing for my history project, Gran. And it's good for you. It's called Reminiscence Therapy.'

'Are you *patronizing* me?'

'Oh, pleeeeeeze, Gran.' I tried some heavy-duty coaxing. 'After all, I *am* your only grandchild. If *I* don't keep the memories alive, who will?'

'Some things are best forgotten.'

When she said that, I felt a coldness creeping into me through a thousand invisible cracks. She didn't mean it, did she? You couldn't just slam the door on everything that had gone towards making you what you were?

Maybe you could. If you had to.

6

The red-haired boy was watching them again. He was supposed to be sweeping the platform, but he swept a whole lot slower when he was sweeping towards them than when he was moving away. Back and forth he went, back and forth, as if in a doze, but he was awake all right. Whenever a train approached, energy rushed into him. His legs trembled as he leaned the broom on the fence and walked briskly, but not hastily, to assist the passengers mounting and alighting. He watched each train until it rounded the bend to the tunnel. Then, with a sigh of resignation, he fetched his broom and started sweeping up after it.

After this last train, as a bonus, there was something thrown down on the platform, the wrapper off a bar of Fry's chocolate. The boy approached it with short, darting stabs, nudging it towards the old brown suitcase on which Emmy and Gus were sitting.

'Tsk! People!' He picked up the wrapper between finger and thumb and dropped it into the bin. 'People!' he said again, louder, and resumed sweeping, crisp with crossness.

Emmy kept her eyes fixed on the spot where the line curved and disappeared from sight. 'Sit tight and wait for Auntie Beattie,' that's what Beryl had told them. And that's what she was doing. Sitting so tightly she was afraid she might crack and fall into pieces.

But Auntie Beattie hadn't come.

'Hungry.' Gus kicked his heels against the scuffed flanks

26

of the suitcase. 'Hungry, 'ungry, 'ungry.' Emmy bared her teeth at him. Too late. The boy was coming back.

'Are you waiting for somebody?' He had an anxious expression, Emmy could hear it without looking. She hated him for his anxious expression.

'Auntie!' said Gus. 'OW!' Didn't he know you couldn't go round telling everybody your business? You never knew what they might do with it.

'Well,' said the boy. 'There's only one more train today, and that's a goods train. She won't be on that, will she? Maybe she's took the bus? Hadn't you better go home, in case?'

Wearily, Emmy got up. She pulled Gus to his feet.

'Here—' The boy put out a freckled hand.

'*Don't!*' They both grabbed at the case at once, and the lid flapped open, and out fell toothbrushes and nightclothes and darned underthings—and Emmy's rabbit made from a sock stuffed with rags. At the sight of him, lying on the platform, all twisted up and dirty and old, with his button-eyes staring, and so shamefully, obviously home-made, Emmy felt a great wave of anguish rise within her, as if all the tears of the world were inside her, clamouring to be let out.

The boy saw the spasm in her face and knelt down, picking up items quickly. His hand closed around Rabbit.

'That's Gus's,' said Emmy. He did not challenge her. She was grateful for that. He shut the lid, stowing Rabbit safely out of sight.

'Up you come, then!' He swung Gus on to his shoulder, and lifted the case with his free hand. 'Which way?'

Mrs Wilcocks had her head out of her front door, like a terrier watching for motor cars through a hole in a fence. She saw them coming, and ducked back inside.

27

'Where's your key?' asked the boy, setting Gus down. Emmy stared at him. She hadn't expected to need one.

'Beryl will be back soon.'

'Are you sure?' He looked at her, his face rucked with concern.

'Yes.' The Whatelys didn't take charity, unless charity was very much bigger and stronger and didn't give them an option. 'You'll be in trouble if you're late back.'

That told him.

She watched him disappear up the street. And was lonely for his anxious expression.

Mrs Wilcocks's front door opened, and she came out, scowling savagely.

'Here.' She thrust something at Emmy. It was a plate with a big doorstep of bread and jam on it. Emmy's mouth filled with saliva. 'For your tea.' She jiggled the plate under Emmy's nose, and her wedding ring, worn thin, slid up and down above the raw red knuckle on her finger. In the passage behind her, Emmy saw Mrs Wilcocks's two sons loitering uneasily. She wondered if they had been among the angry men who had come knocking on a night not long ago.

'We've had our tea.' It was a lie. Emmy was aching with hunger. It made her back hurt and her knees tremble and her throat ache and her head feel tight.

Mrs Wilcocks's face went blank. She must have been really cross.

'Hungry!' bellowed Gus, his cheeks red with rage and disappointment. 'Hungry!'

'Hey!' Beryl came belting down the road towards them, dodging the milkman's horse, showing her garters. 'Stop that! Leave him alone!'

'You ought to be ashamed!' Mrs Wilcocks laid straight into her. 'Leaving bairns this small all day wi' nowt to eat.'

'I've brought them some food.' Beryl had a sodden package under her arm. Emmy knew what *that* was. Yesterday's fish and chips that the shopkeeper couldn't sell. Bile rose in her throat. You'd have to be dying to eat cold fish and chips.

'Anything could have happened. Out on the streets all hours, brought back by strangers—'

'I've been working.' Beryl jabbed at the keyhole with her key. 'What d'you expect me to do?'

'The authorities ought to be told if you can't manage.'

'Tell them, then!' Beryl hustled Emmy and Gus inside and slammed the door. 'What d'you think you're playing at, Em? Why couldn't you stay in the house?'

'We've been waiting for Auntie,' faltered Emmy. 'But she didn't come.'

'How could she? I've only just wrote to her. You've made me look a right fool.'

'She won't tell, will she? She won't get us took away?'

'Nobody's taking anybody away,' said Beryl. 'Not while there's breath in my body.'

'It won't be for long. Just until Mother's on her feet again.' Beryl was edging towards the door of the office as she spoke, feeling behind her for the handle.

'You're not coming back,' said Emmy.

'I've just told you—'

'You're not! You say you will, but you don't mean it!' Emmy made a rush forward, and felt hands drop on to her shoulders. *'Beryl!'*

Beryl was halfway out of the door. Her stricken face hung in the space for a moment like a ghostprint. Then she was gone.

'Well now.' The hands rotated Emmy. 'That was a nice carry-on. And your little brother's been good as gold.'

29

Through blurring eyes, Emmy glared at the sensible, round-toed feet sticking out from under the long grey skirt. There was a lump as big as a bedknob filling up her throat, but the Whatelys didn't cry in front of strangers.

'We'll go up to the dormitory now.'

The toes swivelled themselves through one hundred and eighty degrees and turned into heels. Emmy felt a small hand creep into her own. Gripping it tightly, she followed the briskly alternating heels along corridors and corridors, and up flights and flights of stairs, all smelling of gas from the flaring jets in the walls and strong disinfectant. She did not unstick her eyes from those heels until they arrived in the dormitory. Only then did she allow herself to lift her head and take in the full and terrible truth.

'It'll all look better in the morning. Get yourselves into bed now.'

They were in a small room with two iron beds in it. Each was covered by a grey blanket, with a grey cotton nightgown folded up on the pillow. Next to each bed was a table. On each table was a white enamel jug in a basin and a New Testament. Cleanliness next to Godliness. There was a saucer each with a wooden toothbrush on it, a slice of red carbolic, and a face flannel. Half a towel, cut down and hemmed, hung over the end of each bed.

Emmy poured out some water from one of the jugs and flannelled Gus's face and hands for him. She undressed him and got him into his nightgown. It was miles too big and had the same disinfectanty smell as everything else. He was oddly docile, not even squeaking when she got soap in his eye, or bent his arm back to get it into his sleeve. She washed and changed herself quickly and climbed into her own bed. The sheets were tucked in so tightly, she had to fold the hem of her nightgown over her toes and post herself in like a letter.

'Goodnight, children. Don't forget your prayers.'

Emmy lay, flattened by the tautness of sheet and blanket.

'Do we live here now?' asked Gus, a very small voice in the disinfected darkness.

'Just for now.'

Desolation widened inside her, like a stain. *Shut your lips!* that's what Mother would have said. *Shut your lips and shout sugar!* She pressed her lips together, and her body convulsed as if with a dark and terrible laughter. Tears skidded down the sides of her head, into her ears, making them itch. There'll be marks on the pillow in the morning, she thought, feeling a huge sob struggling in her chest like a trapped bird.

'Emmy . . . are you crying?'

She didn't trust herself to answer. The Whatelys didn't show weakness, and they didn't take charity.

Not even from each other.

7

'It was all charity, of course,' said Gran, twiddling between the tines of a fork with her tea-towel. 'That was the worst part. Having no choice but to take it.'

'It doesn't sound too bad. You hear nightmare stories about being in care.'

'But it wasn't *home*. Home was what Mother made, anywhere at a moment's notice, out of the bits in her hamper. Oh, they *tried* to make us feel normal, they even sent me out to the local school to finish the summer term. But the other kids knew straight away where I was from, and that made it so much worse. As if I'd turned into somebody else overnight and there wasn't a thing I could do about it . . . '

*   *   *

'I'm *not* from the Home.' Emmy stamped her foot. 'My mother's waiting for us back at our house, and she's got a new white pinny, and we've got a piano and a back garden, and we're having pease pudding and savoury ducks for our tea.'

The other children put on superior faces to show that they didn't believe her, and Emmy put on a superior face to show that she didn't *care* if they believed her or not, and the teacher said: 'Emmeline, don't *squint!*' and the next thing she knew, she'd been fitted with spectacles, hideous, wire-framed things that squatted on her nose, like some horrible, goggling insect, and nipped a bright red scar into the bridge. When she looked in the mirror, she wanted to die. With every second that divided her from her mother, she felt herself growing more and more unrecognizable, unlovable, as if she were being forced into a disguise that she couldn't find the buttons to undo.

Every afternoon, she set off in the wrong direction to prove that she wasn't going home to the Home. She would never have gone back at all, if she could have plucked up the courage to ask where the hospital was; but the men in the street, picking up dog-ends, leaning on walls in their shirt-sleeves with their caps pulled over their brows, were all Angry Men, and she hurried by them, keeping her head down. Anyway, she *had* to go back. They'd still got the Son and Heir. That was clever of them.

They got cleverer. A doctor examined them. Big, cold hands. Cold, stinging instruments poked under and pressed down on their tongues. The verdict: 'You haven't been eating properly.' As if they'd done it on purpose.

A car journey. Wrapped in blankets, even though it was midsummer. Now the hospital was even further away.

Another bed in another room smelling of disinfectant. A girl's voice: 'She's awake.'

'Where am I?' *I sound like somebody out of a book*, thought Emmy. Heroines who'd been knocked off bolting horses or bashed by bandits with pistol butts always asked where they were when they woke up. At least, they did in the books Beryl used to bring in from the Penny Library.

'Convalescent Home.' The voice belonged to a small girl in a blue frock with a starched white collar and cuffs and a starched white apron over the top. 'I'm Irene. Get dressed quick, you'll miss breakfast.'

There was a blue frock just the same for Emmy, and a pair of boots under the bed. She put on her new disguise, and followed Irene down to the refectory. To her relief, she immediately spotted Gus's hair sticking up from behind

33

an enormous slab of bread and dripping that took him both hands to hold. Everybody had a plateful of it, beautiful beef dripping, white and salty, with big globs of brown jelly in it. Emmy cut her slice into small squares and chewed each one very slowly, out of habit, to make it last.

'What's wrong with you, then?' Irene wanted to know.

'Nothing. My mother's in the hospital.'

'She gonna die?'

Emmy put down her square of bread, unable to speak or swallow. Guilt sat on her tongue, half-chewed.

'You know what happens to bairns with no parents? They go to the Cottage Homes to be trained for domestic service.'

Emmy hid her face in her cocoa and inhaled its sugary darkness. Hot steam clouded her specs and infiltrated her ears.

'Is she having a bairn?' Irene was unstoppable. 'That's what it is, bet you anything. You'll be Surplus to Requirements now.'

'My mother doesn't need any more children.' Emmy shot Gus a swift, checking glance. Sons and Heirs were fragile things. Mother had lost one before.

'Oh, *doesn't* she?' said Irene. 'You wait. It's the Cottage Homes for you all right. You mark my words.'

A bell rang.

'Here we are!' A woman with a large bosom stuck full of pins and needles gave Emmy a small square of hessian. She selected a needle threaded in blue wool from the armoury on her chest.

'What's wrong, dear? Don't you know how to sew?'

'Yes, Miss . . . but it's got letters on. D.B. I'm E.W.'

'Well, unpick them, you silly! And put in your own!'

34

The stitches were tiny and tight, but Emmy poked and picked and pricked her fingers raw until there was nothing left of D.B. but a few holes. She was just making a start on the E for Emmy when it was dinner-time.

Tripe.

Shapeless and eyeless, it leered up at her from the dish.

'I'll have yours,' offered Irene. 'And you don't want rhubarb and custard neither if you're going to get jabbed.'

'Jabbed?' Emmy said faintly. She'd had enough jabbings for one day.

'They use this great, big needle, full of cold, tingly stuff. Fills up your whole arm. You're sick as a dog after.'

'What's this?' Up trundled the dinner-lady, four foot nothing with big bare arms mottled pink-and-blue like the meat in pork pies. Scooping up a tower of dirty plates, she shooed Emmy out of the refectory and down a corridor smelling of gravy and underarms. 'You'll find out what happens to little girls who don't eat their rhubarb!' She pushed open a door with her bottom and backed into a wall of noisy steam, leaving Emmy prickling all over with terror as if she'd got the sewing teacher's cardigan on inside-out. Moments later, the dinner-lady re-emerged, carrying a dish of something. 'Get this down you!' she ordered.

It was rice-pudding with a golden crust on, thick as the welt on a cricketer's pullover—glorious! Emmy ate up every morsel, from the crackly black skin round the edges where the milk oozed through, to the last creamy, knobbly smear.

She had not realized that charity could taste so good.

At the end of a long lawn, volunteer ladies, enjoying the

speckled shade of large straw hats, were pouring out glasses of home-made lemonade. A nurse sat in a deckchair nearby, knitting and handing out toys from a wooden box.

'What d'you want, pet?'

Emmy was astonished. She'd only come to look.

'A doll, please.' She had never had a doll.

'No dolls left.' The nurse handed up a bear. 'What about Teddy? He growls if you tip him the right way.' Emmy tried several ways, and the bear finally responded with a sort of low groan. He was very old, his body gappy and gristly under the scrubby fur, but he would do. She would not have to walk round on her own. Gus had got in with a gang of small boys and was pretending not to know her. She nuzzled the bear's sun-warmed head, and smelled his carpety smell, and ran her fingertips over the pads on his feet . . .

Poor old bear. How she loved him for all of two hours! Then a bell rang and the ladies started stacking glasses and fastening muslin nets over the jugs of lemonade. As if a wind had changed, all the children began drifting back towards the toy box. Counting stitches with one hand, the nurse stretched out the other for each of the proffered toys, and dropped it back in the box.

'Aren't they to keep, then?' asked Emmy.

'Of course not, pet. They're only temporary.'

She didn't want a toy after that.

In bed that night, and every night after it, Emmy pictured her mother's face, and promised to take care of Gus, and prayed: please, please get better soon. During the day, she went about quietly, as if nothing mattered. She did not want to let anyone down.

One night, she fancied that the face was less clear than it had been. This terrified her. What did it mean? That Mother was dying? Or forgetting them? Was it Emmy's fault? Didn't they deserve to have a mother any more? Were they—what was it Irene said?—Surplus to Requirements?

*　　*　　*

'Surplus to Requirements?' I turned away quickly and switched on the kettle. Wouldn't it be neat if you could cry out of just one side of your face and keep on smiling with the other? Like that kid at school—half of her face froze up, and she had to have artificial tears. 'You should get some of those,' Mum said. 'People will start thinking you're an android because you never cry.' She can be dead sarky sometimes. *Why hasn't she rung?*

'And then, just when I'd given up hope entirely, there was Beryl come to take us away!' said Gran. 'Mother was out of hospital, and Father had found somewhere new for us to live.'

A nice happy ending. Great.

But what about us? I wanted to howl it. Haven't *I* lain awake too, night after night, trying to wish things back together again?

If only she'd leave him alone. The Hag. The Witch. The Barbie-doll. The Toy Girl. He'd come back to us, I *know* he would. Divorce is nothing. Just a piece of paper.

He *can't* marry Sherrylynne. He just *can't*.

8

'You really loved your mum, didn't you?'

Four o' clock and she *still* hadn't rung. I was in a mood to stick knives into myself. I mean, didn't she care *at all* that I hadn't rung her?

'I loved her more than anyone in the world,' said Gran. 'Even your grandad, but that's different. Right up until your mother was born . . .'

'*She*'s not very lovable!'

'Oh, you just think you love your father more because he babys you and tells you you're wonderful.'

Dead Dad dead Dad dead Dad dead Dad. I wolfed down another slice of cake, too fast to taste. See what you've done, Daddy? You've turned me into a big, fat cow.

'Well, I *am* wonderful.'

'Lucky old you! But then, you've never had any competition.' OW! OUCH! More knives. 'I was the one in the middle, I didn't count. But pity's for losers, that's what Pop always said. And that includes self-pity.'

Pity's for losers. Yeah, I thought. I bet Mum's on the phone right this minute, blubbing away to all her friends, asking: Why, why, why? and not listening to any of the answers. Is it any wonder I'd finally lost it and told her what I really thought?

Then I saw her again. The way I'd caught her that first night after Dad moved out. Her bedroom door was open. She had her dress up over her head, and she was struggling to get out of it. I could see her knickers. There was something horrible and grotesque about it, like a bird

38

trapped in a curtain. I had this mad fear that she might break free and flap wildly round the room. But she just hopped about a bit and fell sideways on to the bed. Then she started crying. Crying from inside this bag of material, like a sky-diver tangled inside his parachute, falling, falling . . .

I crept away, ashamed of us both.

Isn't that what you're doing now? Running away?

Don't you *dare* tell me I'm not loyal! I'd have stayed if you'd *asked* me. Didn't I do everything in my power to get Dad back for you? I put you on a diet, got you into the sort of clothes he likes, tried to stop you smoking . . . *Why don't you ring?*

'I just had to work that bit harder for their love than the others did,' Gran was saying. 'But I was so afraid of what she'd think when she saw those wretched glasses. It was bad enough when she saw what else they'd done to me . . . '

*   *   *

'Oh, Em!' Elizabeth Whately gazed in horror at the quartet of peeling scabs like cigarette burns. 'And you had such pretty arms too. Why *four*?'

'The doctor said better a sore arm than a pocky face,' mumbled Emmy. 'He said nobody would ever look at my arms.'

'Not now they won't,' grieved her mother.

'Well, I think it's amazing.' Beryl checked the angle of her hat in the carriage window. 'The whole world's trying to live on eighteen bob a week, and they can keep a place like that going.'

'I'd rather they'd given us the money so we could have managed by ourselves.' Elizabeth Whately pulled Gus on to her knee. 'Fat lot of good it is building us back up just so we can go back to more of the same.'

'It'll be different this time,' said Beryl.

'Yes, well.' Elizabeth Whately sucked a corner of her handkerchief and wiped Gus's face with it. He wriggled with disgust. 'Now remember,' she told him, 'when the man comes round, sit still and keep quiet. You too, Emmy.' They were both still small enough to pass without paying.

'You were lucky, Em,' said Beryl. 'I had to stay at the Sally Army for a shilling a night until Auntie Beattie found me. But you should see her house! She has fresh soap in the bathroom every week—Imperial Leather!'

A shadow flickered across Elizabeth Whately's face. She bent her head and blew into Gus's hair so it would fluff up and tickle her eyelashes and she could smell his baby smell that was like new bread and apples, she told Emmy once. Gus put his hand up to push her away and she made pretend bites at his fingers.

'What d'you think?' Beryl took off her hat and turned her head so that Emmy could admire the pale, naked nape of her neck and her dainty ears. 'It's called a shingle. It's the Very Latest. The ends have to be singed off with a poker.'

'It's nice,' said Emmy. 'Your dress is nice too, Mother.' Elizabeth Whately had on a new outfit, a long dress with a matching coat in an aggressive shade of mustard.

'Your father bought it for me off the market,' she said, with an embarrassed laugh. 'He says we're going up in the world and we've to dress the part. I suppose he meant in front of Beattie.' Again, that faint, uneasy shadow crossed her face. 'I hadn't the heart to say no, he was that pleased with himself. I never could argue with your father.'

'Nobody can,' said Beryl. 'The old man likes his own way too much—there's our old street!' Emmy looked down, and there was Sebastapol Terrace back-to-backing with Fashoda Road, and Mrs Wilcocks in the alley in between lifting her washing to let the coal cart through, and scowling up at the engine as it grumbled by above, gruffly glorious and gleaming black, discharging forests of boiling, murky smoke that smelled like coal fires.

'We're not getting off, are we?' Anxiety stabbed.

'No, silly, it doesn't stop.'

As if it had heard them, the engine made a sudden surge, and the red-haired boy with the great wide broom slid rapidly backwards into the past tense. *Up in the world*, Emmy chanted to herself, picking up the rhythm of the train. UP in the world, UP in the world, UP in the world . . .

'Shall we have our sandwiches that Auntie made?' asked Beryl.

And PLEASE make it go right this time.

The sandwiches, like everything else Auntie Beattie had to do with, were irreproachable. Medium slices of home-baked bread buttered right up into the corners, thick slices of cold lamb, thin slices of tomato, and a twist of salt. There was a flask of tea, exactly sweet enough for everybody's taste, and milk in a separate container, and slices of Wensleydale cheese and cold Christmas pudding individually wrapped in greaseproof paper.

'I never can get my puddings to slice,' complained Elizabeth Whately. 'They always fall to bits.'

'Not enough fat,' said Beryl. 'Auntie Beattie says—'

'Auntie Beattie doesn't have to get the fat for her puddings by melting old bacon rinds under the grill.'

'How many aunts have we got?' asked Emmy, seeing that familiar line deepening between her mother's eyebrows.

'Well!' Elizabeth Whately settled back, smiling again. 'There were *seven* sisters, and their names were: Minnie, Beattie, Peggy, Annie, Franny, Kitty, and Lizzie! Lizzie was the youngest.'

'That's you!' said Gus.

41

'That's me! I was born the year Krakatoa erupted. Eighteen eighty-three. The sky was dark all that summer . . . '

'Tell us how you met Pop,' interrupted Beryl.

'Well, I have to go back a bit . . . '

'To a rainy day—' prompted Emmy.

'—and a sixteen-year-old girl in such a terrible rush to grow up that she never could walk anywhere, she always had to *run*! And one rainy day, when she was running home from work, she slipped and fell all the way down a flight of wet stone stairs, seventy-six in all . . . '

Emmy shut her eyes. She could never bear this bit, the pain, the ugliness, the sound of the bone snapping . . .

'They carried her home and sent for the bonesetter, but her leg never did mend right. So they took her to the Free Hospital and the doctor there broke it and set it again and after that . . . ' Elizabeth Whately tapped her knee. 'This poor old leg was three inches shorter than the other one. My parents were heartbroken, of course. But the doctor said—'

'A man on a galloping horse will never notice!' they all chimed in together.

'Yes!' laughed their mother. 'Of course nobody thought that would ever happen, least of all me. Until one day—'

'A man on a galloping horse came galloping into town!'

'Better than that! On a motor-bike! The first we'd ever seen! He was a commercial artist then, he could blow up any photo as big as you like. So *all* the girls wanted their pictures done. Except me, I was too shy.'

'But your mother gave him your picture, and he fell in love with it!' This was the bit Beryl had been waiting for. 'And when he brought it round, you fell in love right back!'

'Not right away,' admitted their mother. 'To tell the truth, I'd got used to being at home. And Beattie said he'd never make any money, for all his big ideas . . . but he wore me down in the end! He said if he couldn't have me, nobody else would.' She gave a wry smile. 'I expect he thought nobody else would want me with this leg. A couple of titches we are, your pop and me, and it looks like Emmy's going to be as bad. At least *you're* growing tall and straight, Beryl, just like an aristocrat.'

'Oh, can't you just see me?' laughed Beryl. 'Drinking champagne and dancing on taxi cabs!'

So the man on the galloping horse carried away the injured mermaid that he found on the shore, and they lived happily ever after, though she never did learn to walk properly on dry land . . . As Emmy was finishing off the story for herself, the green fields outside went spinning off into the distance and flat, pale sands came rushing past. Crowds of gulls, all facing the same way, stood by pools of wind-stirred water. Others hung in the air, as if pegged on to invisible washing lines, flapping backwards, protesting all the way. The train turned a corner, and the sea came unexpectedly close. Seen so near, it was full of individual disturbances. Waves, like small hands opening and shutting. Light, broken up and jiggling, like quicksilver escaped from a million thermometers. The sun was muffled in a net of mist, but below it, there was such a fierceness on the water that it seemed as if every foundry in the kingdom had emptied out its cauldrons of white-hot steel into the sea.

I could like it here, thought Emmy. I could be safe here and never want to leave . . .

Then the whole thing vanished behind camels' humps of grassy sand and golf links and farmland again and industrial yards where the water was tamed and flat and let into pools between corrugated iron sheds. And there

43

was the station with its fringed wooden canopy, sailing briskly towards them like a white barge.

'WHITE BURN SANDS . . . ' Emmy spelled out the sign. So this was where they were going to live next. But for how long?

'There he is!' Elizabeth Whately hurried ahead of them with her quick, lilting walk of a mermaid on dry land that a man on a galloping horse would never notice. Father stood at the barrier in his best suit and his spats and his bowler hat, swinging his cane like a music hall star. He lifted his wife and whirled her round. She struggled with him, laughing, protesting, clinging on to her hat. He set her down, gave Beryl a squeeze, tweaked Gus's nose and ruffled Emmy's hair.

'Been taking good care of your brother for me?'

She drew back, as she always did when she met him again after one of his absences. Just slightly, not enough for him to notice. To her, he always seemed bigger than real, more clearly pencilled in than other people, his hair so black and his teeth so white (though he was missing a few, like Mother, because of doing without when they were little). It always took a while to get used to him again, he was always something of a stranger.

Beryl put her arm through his. They were old muckers.

'Trolleybus coming!' he shouted. 'All aboard!'

'Well!' he said, pulling out keys with a flourish, like a magician producing flowers from his sleeve. 'This is it!'

'A *shop*?' Emmy goggled. 'We've got a *shop*? What are we going to sell?'

He opened the door. Sunlight turned a segment of whirling dust into a spotlight on an empty stage. He

44

stepped into it, pointing his cane at a pale shape that glimmered through the gloom.

'It's a bike,' said Gus.

'Got it in one!' He whirled off the sheet to reveal a bicycle-shaped mummy trussed up in brown paper. They unpeeled it as eagerly as if it were Christmas, a lady's touring bike with a name all of its own, *Ariel*. It had high handlebars and small, low wheels, 'So ladies can ride with decorum,' said Jack Whately, 'which means not showing their ankles. It's a nippy little model is this, only five pounds—'

'Five pounds!' cried his wife. 'Who's got five pounds to spare in a one horse town like this?'

'They'll spare half a crown a week.' His eyes darkened with determination. 'Give me five years, Lizzie, and I'll be king of this one horse town—if we have to eat the horse in the meantime! We go up or we go under. But I can't do it on my own. You've got to believe in me.'

'Of course I do,' she murmured. 'We all do.'

'Right then!' He gave her a smacking kiss. 'Beryl, here's five bob. Run out and get us all some fish and chips!'

They ate them sitting on their suitcases, straight from the newspaper, hot and stinging and vinegary, the first proper meal they'd had all together in months.

'Freshest fish in the country!' said Jack Whately. 'Jumps straight out the North Sea and into the shops!'

'There's somebody watching,' said Gus.

'In the back, quick!' Jack Whately whipped out his handkerchief, wiped his fishy fingers on it, and smoothed down the springy, tarmacadam-black hair that Emmy loved to comb, when he'd let her. The doorbell coughed. 'Lovely afternoon!' they heard him say. 'Perfect weather for a bike ride!'

Emmy looked round. They seemed to be in a large cupboard.

'There's another room as well,' whispered Mother, sensing her disquiet. 'And a yard and a privy, but we have to share. It won't be for long, I'm sure.' But what did *that* mean?

Jack Whately flung open the door.

'She said she'd definitely think it over! What did I tell you, Lizzie? We're on our way up again! We're on our way!'

*   *   *

'And she *believed* him?'

'For better or worse,' said Gran. 'That's how it was in those days.'

'You mean she had no choice?'

'She'd made her choice. They both had.'

'Wow! Sure was a different world!'

Dead Dad, dead Dad, dead Dad.

9

What am I *playing* at? I can't do this!
I switched off the laptop and pushed it away in disgust. I'd been through some pretty dodgy emotions in the last twenty-four hours, but I'd never thought I could sink this low. I was *jealous*. Can you believe it? Of my own gran! Worse than that, I was jealous of *Emmy*, of somebody who didn't even *exist*, except in Gran's memory and my imagination, which probably meant that she was at least *two* people. And the mad thing was, it was *me* who was bringing her to life! With every word I tapped in, Emmy was becoming more and more real, while *Milly* felt as if she was being attacked by some deranged virus and changed pixel by pixel into a stupid, ugly waste of space.

I needed somebody to write *me* a life.

It was nearly midnight. I could still hear Gran moving about and humming. Lovely Gran. She didn't know the worst yet. She was still living in a world with hope in it. I was going to keep her there as long as I could.

I went to see what she was up to.

She was sitting at her desk, studying something through a magnifying glass. I barefooted up behind her and peeked over her shoulder. It was the torn-up photos. I'd forgotten all about them. She had pieced them back together . . .

There were two of them The first one was Emmy and Gus, no question. Emmy was just as I'd pictured her, Gran and yet not Gran, small and serious, with bunches of ringlets. She had on a white dress with three layers of frills and a sash, and white stockings and ballet shoes, and little white gloves, and a ribbon round her forehead. She was pointing her toe. Gus came up just to her chest. He was choking in a boiled shirt with a stiff collar, and his hair was sticking up, and he had a cross expression and one shoulder higher than the other. They were posed in front of a screen with pictures of ladies in rickshaws on it. A studio portrait.

'*Milly!*' We both jumped so hard there were nearly two sets of skins kicked off like knickers on the carpet. 'You almost gave me a heart attack! Are you all right? I've been so worried about you—'

'It's you and Gus, isn't it?' I cut her off quickly.

'Yes! What d'you think? It was taken just after we came out of the Home. With one of those big mahogany cameras on a tripod. The man had to crouch behind it with a cloth over his head. Gus wouldn't stand still, so he gave him a clout.'

'The clothes are so *sweet*!'

'Second hand. Mother could always get hold of things from somewhere. I remember promising myself: When I grow up, I'm going to have everything new. And then we went and had another war! And your mother, with all that money, thinks she's so clever when she picks up a bargain from the Oxfam Shop.'

'What's this other one?' I wasn't up to talking about Mum.

The second picture was of a family group. The woman was sitting down, holding a baby in a white shawl. She had a long skirt covering her legs, and a high-necked blouse with enormous puffed sleeves that looked as if they'd been blown up with a bicycle pump; and her hair was up in a big double bun, like a cottage loaf. The man stood behind her, with a hand on her shoulder. He had

48

dark hair parted centrally and flattened down and shining as if it had been boot-polished; and he wore a Norfolk jacket and plus-fours (those baggy trousers that come down just below the knee—you see them on golfers in old comic books). There was a little girl beside him, holding a hoop with a bow on it. She had glossy dark ringlets under a white tammy, and a white sailor suit and black woollen stockings and black boots.

'Well, he *has* to be Jack Whately. It's the way he sticks his jaw out, just like you do—'

'I do not!'

'And that's Beryl, and you're the baby, and—'

'Well, that's all *you* know! I wasn't even thought of when this was taken. Beryl's only about seven. That's the first Son and Heir, Alasdair. He died in the 'flu epidemic.'

'Oh, how sad.'

'Mother never really got over it. She kept a little shoe of his in her hamper. She took me and Gus on a shilling excursion once to see his grave. I think she'd had a quarrel with my father or something. She liked to go off sometimes just to frighten him. She took some scones for us to eat and we drank water from an iron cup in the cemetery. Then we went home. It seemed to help her somehow, just to look at the grave. It was so small, you'd have thought it was a pet buried there, or a toy . . .'

'That's terrible.'

'Grief was a fact of life. If you wanted counselling, you went to the vicar and he told you to put up with it. Everyone expected to lose at least one child.'

'So, did the photos get torn up by mistake?'

Gran didn't answer. A horrible thought struck me.

'It wasn't *Mum*, was it? Oh, *no*! It was, wasn't it?'

'Look, Milly, it was a long time ago . . .'

49

Honestly. That was just so *typical*. Mum's never really grown up. She must have been one seriously awful kid.

'But it's a tragedy! You can't make out Elizabeth Whately's face at all! She's torn it right through, both ways. Is this the only one of her you've got?'

'Yes.'

'Oh, well.' I tried to be positive. 'You'll always have her in your memory.' I mean, lame or what?

'We had this one enlarged.' Gran was trying to change the subject. 'To advertise Father's skills as a commercial artist. Everybody wanted a picture of their parents for the front parlour. That's where people used to sit on a Sunday. It was a treat just to have a different view out of the window.'

'I thought you were going to sell bikes?'

'Yes, but until that first bike went, we couldn't order another one. And we had to eat. Luckily the rent wasn't much. Landlords were practically giving premises away with so many tenants doing moonlight flits! Father did the pasting and framing, and Mother filled in the eyelashes and small details with charcoal. I can still see her . . . I can *still* . . . ' Gran put a hand up to her eyes. ' . . . buttoning up her long green overall . . . going to stand behind the counter . . . waiting for somebody to come in with a half crown deposit . . . '

'Gran? Are you OK?'

'It's no good, Milly!' She looked up at me with a desperate expression. 'I could *always* see her. Wherever I was, whatever I was doing, she was *always* there when I needed her. And now she's gone.'

'Your mother? You mean, like when you were in the Home?'

'Yes.'

'Then it's only temporary.'

'I feel so ashamed.'

'Gran, all you need is some kind of a trigger! That's how your memory works. There's always a back-up, even if you wipe the file by mistake.'

'Yes . . . yes, you're right.' She tried to look convinced. 'Thanks, Milly. You're a good kid. I hope your mother appreciates you.' She stood up. 'And now, I really must go to bed. D'you want anything? A hot drink or anything?'

'No thanks.'

She's getting smaller, I thought, as I watched her moving away down the hall.

But getting forgetful? Not Gran. If Gran ever goes to pieces, we've all had it.

Something drifted up to the surface. One of those all-night sessions, when Mum had wanted to go on and on about why Dad didn't love her any more. I'd come up with every answer I could think of, every possible reassurance, and she still wasn't satisfied. 'I don't want solutions, Milly,' she'd yelled at me. 'I just want somebody to *listen*, to really *listen*, while I work it out for myself. Or else I'm never going to get through this and move on.'

'If you'd spent more time listening to Dad, maybe he wouldn't have dumped you.'

I didn't say it. Not then.

'You just want me to shut up and go to bed,' she said balefully. 'You think if you can tidy it all away, you can stop it happening. It doesn't work like that.'

She was right. I was scared of her pain. Embarrassed by it. And anyway, I didn't want her to move on.

But she had to go and blow it, didn't she?

That's what last night was all about.

So *that's* when I said it. *All* of it.

I didn't have any difficulty picturing *her* face. Too much make-up, a few red veins on the cheeks from too many glasses of Chardonnay, her hair dropping down from a strandy bun. I couldn't imagine never being able to see it. Why don't you *ring*, you old Moo? You *never* hold out this long. All right, you drive me barking, but we have a laugh, don't we? Nobody else has our sense of humour. *Ring, damn you!* I'm ready to forgive you. So *why don't you*—?

The phone rang.

I grabbed it.

'Hello—is that my Millybird?'

I couldn't speak. Couldn't move.

It was Dad.

10

'Is that you, Millybird?' He was using his special name, his caring voice, the coward, the toad, the hypocrite. 'Talk to me, Millybird. Tell me you forgive me.' I had to hold on to the table. My legs were rattling like a couple of drinking straws. 'Darlingest Milly, you know I never wanted to hurt you . . .'

But you *did*! I wanted to scream it into the mouthpiece. You hurt me, you *really* hurt me, every minute, every second, every nano-second for a whole *year*, and I didn't mind, I didn't care, I forgave you, even when you started bringing Sherrylynne Skinnybones round, even when you expected me to let her share Our Time, because I thought it was just a thing you were going through, something that happens to men when they get scared of growing old and dying, and I'll forgive you again, all over again, if you'll only forget her and put things back the way they were . . .

'. . . but I can't change the situation, Milly, and I don't want to.' Rage flooded my mouth, worse-tasting even than pot noodle, even than oil of cloves, the worst taste in the world, the taste of toothache. 'You've been so wonderfully supportive . . .' The room filled with the smell of burning toenails. '. . . and I know I can rely on you to keep on coming up with that support. Because you're not a child any more, are you, Millybird?' I was gripping the receiver so tightly, the plastic squeaked in my ear. 'You're a young woman. A lovely, sensitive, sensible, caring young woman. So, what say we pick you up tomorrow morning and all go out for the day? Just the three of us? Millybird?'

I needed to swallow, but I couldn't get the muscles to work. My throat seemed to be made out of egg box material.

'At least you're listening. I knew Joanna was making too much of it. But we know what she's like, don't we?' And he laughed, he actually *laughed*. 'And we won't breathe a word to your gran if that's a problem, OK?' Then he said some other stuff that I can't tell you about yet, I just can't, it's too sick-making. 'Shall we say ten o'clock? Do I take it that's a yes?'

I put down the phone. I couldn't let go of the table. I felt so vague and weird and scared. And *angry*. I couldn't believe his arrogance. Assuming, just *assuming* he could get round me with a few sugary words. And what was all that stuff about me being an adult? I'd always been his Millybird. Was I an instant grown-up now, just to suit *them*?

'Who was that?' Gran put her head round the door.

'Mum. She sends her love.' Out rolled the lies as easily as defrosted pastry. That's regular practice for you.

Then it hit me. The brainwave.

'Gran, let's go to White Burn Sands! Now! OK, *not* now—tomorrow, first thing!' This is it, this is *it*. Get away from them, far away, if they can't catch up with us, they can't make it real.

'What for?'

'To get your mother's face back!'

'Oh, Milly, do you really think—?' She looked so eager, so excited, that just for that moment, I honestly believed I was doing it for her as much as for me. 'But it's such a terribly long way. Hundreds of miles.'

'So what? We're on holiday.'

'If only you could drive . . . '

'I know enough for an emergency. The old man took me round the car park a few times. It's easy.'

I lay in bed, waiting for it to be time to get up, scared that Dad would arrive early and prevent our escape. I couldn't let him ruin it for Gran. It was Gran who was important, I told myself that over and over.

I got up at six to tidy the flat for burglars. Gran wouldn't set foot outside unless everything was just so. I looked up White Burn Sands in the road atlas—it was a lot further than I'd thought—and made some sandwiches. The more I got done, the more committed she'd feel. That was the theory, anyway.

'Oh, Milly! We weren't serious, were we?' Gran came in in her dressing-gown.

'Do it for me.' I couldn't let her waste time arguing. 'Essential research. You want me to do well in my GCSEs, don't you? I've got the route sorted and everything.' The kettle beeped. I poured boiling water on to a tea bag and went to plug in the Hoover.

'Milly! Put some shoes on! You should never do housework in bare feet!'

'I'm not going to get electrocuted.' I fished out the tea bag with a spoon. 'There's a trip-out switch in the fuse box, didn't—YOUCH!' The boiling tea bag slid off the spoon and plopped on to my naked foot. I tried to kick it into the pedal bin and the lead from the Hoover went snaking away over the table top. Before I could get clear, the plug pounced down and smacked on to the knuckles of my other set of toes. 'SHUGGA!'

'My, we are in a panic,' said Gran, peeling open one of my sandwiches and inspecting the contents. 'Anyone would think we were going on the run.' She picked up a knife and started to scrape off the butter. 'How many more times, Milly? Spread it *thinly*. Waste not, want not.'

Great start. Mugged by an appliance. I limped out, dragging the Hoover behind me. It wasn't about to be tamed. It mauled the bath mat so savagely that I had to turn it round to hide the chewed bits. When I was nozzling behind the sofa on my hands and knees, it sucked up the end of my T-shirt and nearly throttled me. Then the upright bit fell over and cracked me on the back of the skull. I suppose I was lucky it didn't slurp out one of my eyes and make me waste another ten minutes fishing it back out of the bag.

It was *nine o'clock* by the time we got going. I was convinced Dad's Range Rover was going to come muscling up at any second, but there's no hurrying Gran. She just sets her jaw and takes even longer. Calm under fire, that's what being Emmy had taught her to be.

I thought she'd never finish the cockpit drill. She checked her seatbelt and mine and the doors and all the mirrors—as if they'd be any different from the day before! She even got out a tissue and *polished* the rear view one!

'Leather and petrol!' she said, smiling blissfully as she finally started up the engine. 'The smell of luxury! That's what Father always used to say. He taught our Beryl to drive. You didn't have to take a test in those days.' She frowned, feeling for the bite. 'It's only taken me sixty-odd years to catch up.' She checked over her shoulder and let off the handbrake. We started to move. At last.

'Traffic's not too bad. Reckon it should take four hours tops once we get on the motorway.'

'Motorway?' said Gran.

'Coming up in a minute. See the signs?'

'Ah,' said Gran.

56

'You'll be able to put your foot down then.'

'Mmmm.'

She took forever waiting for a space to slot in.

'You can go now, Gran. Go, go, go! That's it!'

'Was that right? Do I stay in this lane, or what?'

I checked her sideways face, crinkled with concentration, like a ginger nut.

'You *have* been on a motorway before, haven't you, Gran?'

'Well . . . there's never been any call to.'

This was a big, big mistake, said a voice in my head.

'Should I stop for this lad?'

'Not on the motorway! He shouldn't be there! Don't slow down!'

The red-haired boy's head flicked round as we passed him, and our eyes met. I felt snatched by something, a sense of recognition. I watched him in the mirror, growing smaller and smaller, his hand half raised. Like a signpost.

I think I knew then that we hadn't seen the last of him.

I think that's when I chose him.

11

'If we can just hold on until Christmas,' Gran was saying. 'Then it was: if we can just hold on until Easter . . . That's how Pop got us through it. And for my eighth birthday, I got a lucky sixpence all of my own! To spend, not to save! We went to the picture-house, and I saw my first film, *The Phantom of the Opera*, the silent version, of course.'

'It was a hip kind of a town, then?'

'Don't mock, Milly! It doesn't become you. We had our share of excitements. We even had the Prince of Wales visit our school, the one who abdicated to marry that scraggy old woman. We were all lined up to wave our Union Jacks in the rain.'

'What was he like?'

'A funny, ratty little man in a greatcoat. He kept his eyes on the ground the whole time. Couldn't wait to get back to his hotel. When the sun came out, he played a round of golf on the links. Then he got on his yacht and sailed away . . . '

*   *   *

'And they get you all singing "Land of Hope and Glory" on Empire Day,' snorted Jack Whately. 'Fat lot of good having an empire ever did any of *us*.'

A bigger treat was a visit to the local museum, where the star exhibit was a model of a piece of cheese with a fly on it as a warning against germs.

Soon after this, Jack Whately found a big double-fronted

shop nearer the centre. It had belonged to a high-class grocer, who'd gone bust, 'pushed out by the Pile it High and Sell it Cheap merchants. Still, their loss, our gain.'

'They might have left us the counter,' grumbled Elizabeth Whately. 'It was a lovely piece of mahogany.'

'They've left the fixtures.' Jack Whately rattled his cane along the bank of drawers filling up the back wall.

'Only because they couldn't shift them.'

Emmy clambered through the heaped rubbish and pulled open one of the little drawers by its brass handle. A smell of ghostly raisins wafted out. She tried another. Each one released the spirit of something different and delicious—peppermint, pennyroyal, lemon-thyme, cloves . . .

'Gus has got in the cellar!' shouted Mother. Emmy hurried after him. The dust on the iron rail under her hand was thick and soft as felt. A murky light from a window level with the feet of people in the street revealed a jumble of tins, jars, barrels and boxes, thrown all together.

'Biscuits!' crowed Gus. But they were so stale, Emmy could push a finger into them up to the knuckle. Several giant boxes of chocolates turned out to be dummies. They traipsed back upstairs and helped Mother to feed a fire in the big room at the back of the shop. It took two weeks to get rid of all the rubbish.

Elizabeth Whately re-wrote all the labels on the little drawers, and the aromatic recesses were soon filled up with an assortment of cotter-pins, pumps, lamps, bells, and bits of valve-rubber. Meanwhile, Jack Whately made his own counter out of empty crates, and pasted it all over with advertisements.

'Who's to know it isn't mahogany?'

The next thing he wanted was a sign over the shop door. Black lettering on a white background: J. A. WHATELY & SONS.

'You've only got one son,' Emmy pointed out.

'It's just what people put,' said Mother.

The painter came on an ancient, trembling bicycle with his ladder over his shoulder. He whistled as he worked, but Emmy saw how his hand shook with terror in case he made a mistake. She wondered where her father would find the money to pay him. But nobody ever saw Jack Whately's hand trembling.

*   *   *

'He was a bit of trend-setter, wasn't he?' I checked the mirror for Range Rovers. 'Selling on credit, I mean.'

'Oh, the church didn't approve one bit!' chuckled Gran. 'They saw it as money-lending. But it's no different from saving up, and you got the goods almost at once. It was mean what the manufacturers did, though. They made us put up a notice: NO CREDIT TO MINERS OR DOCKWORKERS. They said casual men couldn't be relied on to keep up the payments.'

'So a miner or a docker couldn't have a bike?'

'Or a radio or a watch. Not on credit, anyway. There was a bit of spite in there, I reckon, after the Strike. The bosses liked to remind them of their place. My friend Elsie Page was a dockworker's kid. She used to get let out of school early to run up the Dock Road with her dad's dinner-pail. She could have done with a bike.'

'OK, OK, tell me some more about Elizabeth Whately.'

'What sort of thing?'

'First thing that comes into your head.'

'Oh, I can't! It's too much like a quiz, I don't know what I'm supposed to—nasturtiums!'

'Pardon?'

'Nasturtiums!' said Gran triumphantly. 'Mother missed having a garden terribly, so she prised up a row of cobbles in the yard and planted nasturtium seeds. They make a lovely show. You can eat them as well, but they're a bit peppery. I was so impressed, I bought some flower bulbs when I had some money and put them in a pot in the back of a cupboard. I wanted so much to be like her . . . ' She fell silent for a moment, smiling to herself, and when the smile faded, I knew what she had been doing: searching for that forgotten face under the scar-tissue of a torn photograph. But she hadn't found it.

'Something else, quick. Four fast facts.'

'Erm . . . '

'Something she said?'

'You never see sea captains with bad eyes! I'd completely forgotten that! It was just after we came to White Burn Sands. She took me and Gus to find the beach, so I could practise looking at the horizon like a sea captain. But after we'd gone a few blocks, her leg was hurting so badly, she gave up. ''I'm too old for beaches,'' she said. So we went on our own. I know what you're trying to do, Milly, and it's not working.'

'Another fact, quick! Don't stop to think about it!'

'All right, all right! She was upset when she found Gus folding up his own clothes, because he'd learned how to do it in the Home.'

'Good! Next!'

'Er—she had a dent in her thumb-nail where a sewing-machine needle went right through it and out the other side.'

'OW!'

'I liked to run the tips of my fingers over the scar on the other side of her thumb, on the fleshy bit.'

'Ow! Ow! *Ow!* Next!'

'Can we give it a rest? I can't concentrate on the road if you get me all het up.'

'OK, OK.' Maybe it wasn't such a good idea to try

kick-starting somebody's memory in the middle of a four-lane motorway.

We drove on in silence for a few minutes. Then—

'Her parlour window . . . ' said Gran, almost to herself.

'Sorry?'

'Her parlour window over the shop. She used to sit there on Sundays. Pop would be downstairs, waiting for somebody to come in for a penn'orth of valve-rubber, and she'd be up there, watching the afternoon strollers. She loved that parlour. It took her years to get it just how she wanted it. When business really started to pick up, and we were ordering twenty bikes a week, the manufacturers sent somebody round to check us out, so we carried all Mother's best furniture downstairs and put it in the room behind the shop to make a good impression. That's where we spent most of our time. After he'd gone, we had to carry it all back up again! I always used to glance up at that window when we were walking back from Sunday school, and there she'd be, gazing out . . . '

'Well, that's it!' I said. 'That's *it*!'

'What's it?'

'We'll find the window. And *that's* where we'll find her face!'

12

The red-haired boy was still watching me. I double-checked in the mirrored panel behind the optics while I was queueing for coffee. The boy from the motorway. When he saw he'd been sussed, he didn't look away. He smiled, just with his eyes. I stared back coldly, like you do. Never give in first.

'That'll be one ninety-eight,' said the girl on the till.

'What?'

'Two coffees. One-nine-tee-eight-pee.'

'Sorry.' It gave me an excuse to break the eye-lock. I collected my sachets and plastic spatulas, and headed back to Gran.

I was having twinges of guilt about Mum, which was deeply irritating, considering that everything, without exception, was entirely her fault. I mean, she just wouldn't *try*. She should have been able to see off an airhead like Sherrylynne in five minutes flat. It's like she just gave up. 'But it's *happening*, Milly,' she kept saying. 'How will I ever get used to it, if you won't let me face facts?'

Well, she was having to face them now.

Gran had bagged a table outside and was shelling hard-boiled eggs into a napkin.

'Why did that aunt of yours pray in the bathroom? If that's what she was doing?'

'Auntie Franny?' said Gran. 'She had twin boys, and they both died. She couldn't get over it, so her husband left her. She had to go into hospital. That's where she ''got religion'', to comfort herself, I suppose.'

'What happened to her?'

'She lived with Auntie Beattie for a while, then she rented a couple of rooms and took in ironing. We visited her once. She used to put newspaper over the fender, so it wouldn't rust. Funny the lives people end up with . . .'

'Some people do all right.' I took a savage bite of my egg and black-peppered the bite-marks. Amazing how anger sharpens the appetite. 'Men do, anyway.'

'The working-man's word is law in his own house.'

'Sorry?'

'That's something else Mother said. I can even remember what she was doing when she said it—cutting the arms out of a pullover to make a pair of socks! I'd just come in all upset because Elsie Page and I had both passed to go to the High School, and Elsie had got a free place, but her dad wouldn't let her go because he couldn't afford the uniform. So then Beryl wanted to know why he should have it all his own way, and Mother said, "Because he's a slave everywhere else. That's why they invented wives . . ."'

'Your dad wasn't a slave.'

'He was a slave to the bank.'

'Well, he must have been doing all right if he could afford school fees. How much were they?'

'Nine pounds a year—an absolute *fortune*! We'd been in the town three years by then and were just about holding our own, but it must have been a struggle. I remember him giving me a twenty pound note once, just to hold, in case I never got the chance again . . .'

'I bet he was proud of you.'

'Oh, it was like a miracle! Suddenly I was somebody in my own right. I was the clever one. But it's no wonder

Elsie's dad put his foot down. When we saw the list of stuff the school expected us to buy . . . '

*   *   *

On the first day of the holidays, Emmy went with Mother to the School Store, a narrow, high-ceilinged establishment smelling of beeswax and barathea. The sales assistant looked like a headmistress, with grey hair in a bun, keys at her waist and pince-nez pincering her nez.

'Are you buying for the Convent, or for the High?'

'The High School, please,' said Elizabeth Whately. The assistant released a discreet smile of approval.

'Shall we begin with the gym slip?'

'We'll just look at badges for the time being.'

Emmy shot her mother an apprehensive glance. Badges were things you couldn't buy anywhere else. She felt a tiny cooling of her excitement, and a faint sense of dismay. The badges duly arrived, big ones, small ones, middle-sized ones, badges for every item of clothing, even the knickers! Then there was the school tie, the house tie, the scarf, the girdle (a sash made out of braid), and the hats: a blue serge cap for winter, a panama for summer, and a black velour hat with a band on for special occasions.

'That'll do.' Elizabeth Whately snapped her purse shut. 'We'll get everything else in town.' She meant *cheaper*.

'You'll not find our gym knickers anywhere else,' sniffed the assistant. 'The pocket is a unique feature.'

'I dare say we could put a pocket on for ourselves, couldn't we, Em?' Emmy tried to smile. But deep inside, in a shameful, secret place, a mutinous voice whispered: This is my new start. Why can't we do it *properly*?

'Well, of course the whole idea of a uniform,' said the assistant, 'is uniformity. Any girl at the High wants to be *seen* to be from the High.'

'I thought she was going there to improve her mind,'

rejoined Elizabeth Whately. 'I hope folk'll be able to spot any improvement in that area without having to check what drawers she's got on. Good afternoon!'

Shoe shopping next. Black lace-ups for winter, patent-leather pumps with a bar across for summer, canvas shoes for gymnastics. The ones in the School Shop had toe-caps and were one and eleven, but in Marks and Spencer's you could get them without toe-caps for a shilling. 'Madness to pay more!' declared Mother. But the secret voice whispered how much it would have liked toe-caps. And the gym-slip from Marks and Spencer's was a *bargain* at four and eleven. But the one in the School Shop had deeper pleats . . .

They shopped until they were loaded like Christmas trees. Emmy felt as if they had gone out and bought a whole new life for her to grow into.

'No need to tell your pop we've cut a few corners,' said Mother. 'You know how proud he is, even though he's the first to shout if he thinks he's been rooked.'

Gus watched the parcels being unwrapped. He was very quiet during supper. As soon as he could, he went off to his private cubby-hole upstairs.

Next morning, when Emmy went to the cupboard to water her plants, she found that somebody had taken a pair of scissors and snipped the new green shoots off every one . . .

*   *   *

'He was jealous, I suppose. For the first time in his life, you were the important one.' Through my eyelids, kinked against the sun, I felt sudden shameful tears of jealousy breaking. Of whom? Faceless, shapeless yet. The Usurper.

'I suppose so.' Gran drew a long sigh. 'I just wish I hadn't had all those wicked thoughts. Mother was trying so hard to stretch the pennies. I hope she never guessed.'

Wicked thoughts? If those were the wickedest thoughts she'd ever had, it was a good thing Gran couldn't see inside my head. I pulled my hair over my ear to be on the safe side.

'What did you get for your nine pounds, then? Latin and Greek?'

Gran laughed.

'Washing!'

'Washing? What d'you mean? Brains? Drugs money?'

'You needn't sound so superior. It was an important subject for a girl. We were all going to be wives and mothers—don't look like that! Everybody pitied spinsters. There were no single mums—not out in the open, anyway—and even if we didn't do the laundry ourselves, we'd have to supervize the maids. We had to bring Rinso Powder, blocks of red and white washing soap, and something to wash. The teacher held up this enormous pair of bloomers with elasticated legs. "This is the sort of thing you should be bringing, gels!" We didn't know where to look.'

'Did you say *maids*?'

'Oh, yes. Lots of the girls had them. It was a bit of a culture shock. They lived in a different world from us, up by the park, in avenues and boulevards, not streets. Their houses were detached. It was one of the maids who told my friend Dottie the facts of life. Then Dottie told them to me. That was my sex education! What *is* that anyway? I mean, what do you find to talk about week after week?'

'Oh . . . you know.'

'Well, it obviously doesn't work. Your mother said there were five pregnancies in your school last year.'

There were a lot more than five, if you believed all the rumours, but I wasn't getting into that. Gran meant there were five babies.

'Yeah. The Moo-Cows.'

67

'*Milly!*'

'That's just what we call them. They're the no-hopers. The ones who can't think of anything else to do with their lives. They all say they're going to go to college, but everybody knows they won't.'

'Anybody can slip up.'

'Nobody *has* to.' I almost bit her head off. 'That's one thing they *do* teach us.'

We were back in dark and sharky waters.

'I didn't know you had such strong opinions,' said Gran.

'We'd better get going,' I said.

13

'Can't we stop this time, Milly? Before we get out into the traffic? He's only a youth.'

'All hitchhikers are psychopaths, Gran. *Don't slow down!* It's horrible when people do that and then speed up again. It's like they're checking you out and deciding you're not pretty or interesting enough.'

'How would you know? Don't answer that. You children take such terrible risks.'

'He's not a child. You just fancy him because he's got red hair. He's all right, anyway, there's a wagon stopping.'

The lorry drew level with us not long after. The boy from the service station was perched in the cabin high above us with his feet on the dash. I was glad we hadn't picked him up. He'd made me uneasy, the way he looked at me. He wasn't looking this time. That annoyed me like mad.

'I always worry about children,' said Gran. 'I still worry about your mother. Just like she worries about you.'

'She's got no reason to.'

'It goes with the job. I've seen how she looks at you when you're being so brave and sensible—'

'And how's that?'

'As if she wishes you'd break down once in a while, so she could do something to help.'

'I don't need any help.'

'Couldn't you pretend, sometimes?'

'Look, just because I don't want to mope around with

a lot of egos pretending to be victims—they don't really *care* about each other. Give me another fact about Elizabeth Whately.'

'Oh, not *that* again! I'm no good at this.'

'Yes you are. Come on. Four instant, invigorating images!'

'You sound like your father.'

'I do NOT!'

'All right, all right, let me think . . . Oh, this is so typical of her, Milly. I came in one day and found her kneeling on the kitchen floor with a poor, poisoned puppy in her arms. She was lowering it into a basin of warm water to try and soothe its agony.'

'Somebody *poisoned* your dog?'

'Unbelievable, isn't it? They threw bad meat over the fence. That was when we were just starting to get known. We'd got on too fast, people said. And of course there was me, going out every day in my new school uniform . . . You'd have thought we'd committed a crime. We'd got on because we'd *had* to. Is this our exit?'

'Yep.'

We didn't speak while she negotiated it.

'Anyway, most of it was just putting on a front. We used to tell everybody we'd got all our carpets from Dibbs's, the posh department store. It was *sort* of true. They auctioned off strips of their own carpet, the bits that had been under the counters and along the walls and hadn't got trodden on much. We did all downstairs with it, it was lovely and springy—'

'Let's get back to Elizabeth Whately.'

'Oh. Right. Well . . . she used to lock herself in the bedroom when he'd been drinking. He wasn't violent, but we all hated what it did to him, so we kept out of his way. She'd signed the pledge when she was fifteen so she never drank.'

'Not even at Christmas? Yeah—tell me about Christmas!'

'Christmas was never a good time for us.'

'Why not?'

'It just wasn't. There's that lad again! It's all right to stop here, isn't it? I'm going to anyway.'

'Are you sure?' he said, stooping to look in the window.

Pale, greeny-grey eyes, with crinkles round them from spending the summer out of doors. Sandy-reddish hair, with bits of gold in, like the shreds in finely-cut marmalade. Thin, straight nose. Teeth not so good. I wasn't looking, you understand. I was staring dead ahead so he'd know he was dealing with Gran, not me, that this wasn't my idea at all.

'You're not a psychopath, are you?' said Gran. He grinned, shaking his head. His breath smelled of chewing-gum and rolling tobacco. 'Where are you heading?'

'Newcastle way.'

I sensed a fractional resistance, but she overcame it.

'Hop in, then.'

I got out to let him into the front. I had this mad idea that if he pulled a knife or something, I could hit him from behind.

'Push your seat back,' Gran told him. 'Give yourself more room.' He had long legs, long thighs, like cabers. 'Milly won't mind. She's only got little legs.'

Duh! Thanks a bunch, Gran.

'Is Newcastle your home?' she asked, pulling away.

'Nah. I left when I were two.' He hadn't lost his accent though.

'What brings you back?'

I watched his hair, the bit I could see round the head

71

rest, lifting and flopping in the movement of air, as if with the effort of his thinking.

'Chasing faces,' he said, after a moment. 'Aye.' He was pleased with his definition. 'That's what I'm doing.'

'I'm sorry?'

'I thought it were time I met them all, like. The rest of the family. Let them know how I'm getting on. I'm going to university in September.'

'Oh, well done!'

'Thanks. I'm Dominic, by the way.'

'I'm Emmy.' That startled me. 'And this is my grand-daughter—'

'Hi, Milly.' He turned his head and smiled, and his pale eyes said *I know all about you*. It's a cheap trick. Guys do it all the time. It's supposed to make you feel all weak-kneed and helpless. All it really means is they think you're no different from any other chick. But it was unnerving all the same. As if he knew it was *me* who had willed him into the car . . . He turned back to Gran. 'You headed for Newcastle too?'

'No. We don't know it at all.' I was shocked. It was the first time I'd ever heard Gran tell a bare-faced lie. Maybe she thought he was descended from one of the Angry Men. 'We're going to White Burn Sands.'

'I *thought* I picked up a bit of a twang.' That'll nark her, I thought. Gran prides herself on not having an accent.

'Really?' She didn't seem to mind. 'I haven't been back for years! Actually . . . we're chasing faces too, aren't we, Milly?'

I couldn't believe it. Telling him our private stuff.

'Is that right? You can overtake this Cortina, Emmy. Ease out . . . that's it. Foot down—Great!'

'I did it!' crowed Gran. 'I did it! I overtook!'

72

'Your first time? Why, that's brilliant, man! Keep your foot down now. We've a way to go yet.'

And he just took over. I was furious. OK, maybe a tad relieved as well. At least there was a chance now that we might reach White Burn Sands in one piece and before dark.

He slammed the car door and stood for a moment, looking round, his eyes slitted and secretive in the bright sunshine. He was older than I'd thought. Not a kid at all. A man. With big, sharp shoulders, hunched slightly, as if in a shrug. He felt me looking and smiled, not the mocking, knowing smile from the car, but a self-mocking, self-knowing smile that said: *I'm a bad lad. We both know it, don't we? But you don't care. You like it.* An arrogant humility.

He was a lot taller than me. I had to look up at him. I didn't like that. It made me feel like some kind of adoring little poodle or something.

'Shall we have tea this time?' Gran was feeling in her handbag. '*Somebody* forgot the flask.' What did she have to bring *that* up for? 'Not to mention the map.'

'I made notes, didn't I? We haven't got lost yet, have we? It's all right, I've got money.' I didn't like the hungry, sideways look Dominic was giving her purse.

He ambled along beside me to the cafeteria, taking two strides to my three.

'Have I done summat to annoy you?' he said.

We moved along the queue.

'You're not going to university at all, are you? You needn't bother to lie. Gran doesn't believe you either. She's just being nice.'

'No, I'm not. I never got any exams.'

I felt bad then.

'It's not too late. Plenty of people do it later these days. They reckon mature students have more staying power.'

'Do they?' He was laughing at me. I wished I'd kept my mouth shut. Men do that, laugh at you. It's to panic you, make you wonder what you've said that's stupid.

'Are you in the habit of telling lies?' I asked.

'Aren't you?'

'I beg your pardon?'

'Haven't *you* got a secret face? One you don't show anybody?'

'In your dreams.' I grabbed a couple of packs of sandwiches and dropped them on to the tray. 'Three teas, please.' My voice sounded high and unnatural. He watched me pay, and picked up the tray for me. He had big, sunburned hands with slightly swollen fingers, from doing some sort of labouring work, maybe, and dirty fingernails. I was shocked by what came into my head. I mean, one minute you're in deepest mourning for your lost life, and the next—'I can manage, thanks.' I tried to take the tray from him. My fingers brushed his and jumped away as if I'd plugged them into a light socket.

He smiled again.

Gotcha.

14

I made for the loo fast. I reckoned I could trust him not to mug Gran while I was away. Just.

There was a spot on my chin that looked as if it had eaten about a million Mars Bars. I could have howled. Of course I'd felt it prickling up in the car. I must have been fondling and fingering it without thinking. Had Dominic noticed? How could he *miss* it? It was taking over my entire face. *That's your fault, Dad.* I gave it a little squeeze to be sure—Spit! Spot! A zit-squirt! A spite-spurt! There's nothing so bad that you can't make it a real stinker if you put your mind to it.

I lathered it with make-up and strolled back to the others, trying to look unconcerned.

'Is that a spot on your chin?' said Gran. I wanted to vaporize with humiliation. 'What's that stuff you've put on it?'

'Concealer,' I muttered, feeling my whole face reddening and swelling into one gigantic septic blob.

'That'll just make it worse. What you want on that is a small, neat square of sticking-plaster.'

'Why don't I strap a lamp to my head? And a notice—This way to the grotto!' Dominic grinned, and I felt a little bit better. But not much.

'Everybody gets spots in their teens. Your mother *still* gets spots. That's because she's always dieting and she wears too much make-up. So be warned.'

'I'm not on a diet.'

'All this faddy food, that's what wrecks your skin.

75

Plain, ordinary food that keeps you regular . . . ' Oh, *God!* She wasn't going to start talking about *bowels*, was she? Other people's grandmothers did that, not *mine*. ' . . . that's the stuff you want.' She bit into a sandwich. 'Ugh! What's this?'

'Tuna and sweetcorn.'

'It's like eating bubble-wrap! Bubble-wrap and fish-paste sandwiches!' They were laughing at me, ganging up. 'And to think, we were so dreadfully poor that Mother used to buy some fruit and put it in a bowl in the window at Christmas just to show people we could afford some. We weren't allowed to eat it.'

'Bit of a waste of money, then,' I snapped. 'What did you cure your spots with? Coaldust and toothpaste?'

'Boracic powder and lard,' said Gran promptly, and I had to smile. You couldn't make up stuff like that. But it had been a close thing. We'd very nearly quarrelled. For the first time ever, and in front of a total stranger. Get a grip, Milly.

'I was just telling Dominic how many people I knew who lived upstairs. Like my friend Thora from the Girls' Guild. She lived in two rooms up a stair. Every drop of water had to be carried in and out, and the place was running with damp! I went to call for her once, and she was unravelling a jumper. Next time I saw her, she was knitting it into a bathing costume. That's how poor they were.'

'Woollen bathing-costumes?' said Dominic.

'Ooh, they were horrid! As soon as you got in the water, they went all soggy and sank down round your waist. You were in real trouble if you had any kind of a bust.'

'What was the Girls' Guild?' He was asking all the questions *I* should have been asking. First he'd taken over Gran; now he was trying to take over Emmy. What was going on?

'Oh, we used to put on concerts. Tap dancing, that sort of thing.'

Wake up, Gran! *Log on!* Can't you see what a *creep* he is?

'Are you going to call your mother?'

'What?' I hadn't realized the story was over. Something about somebody hanging themselves in the back of their sweetshop because they couldn't make the business pay, and Jack Whately saying, 'You go up or you go under', and Emmy picturing the man gasping and choking, drowning in air from the end of the banisters . . .

I hadn't really been listening.

I'd been trying to outstare Dominic. I hadn't got into it on purpose. I'd caught his eye by accident, and looked away, and looked back when I thought I wouldn't get caught. And got caught.

Of course I knew all the techniques he was using. They'd already been road-tested on me by all those poor, pathetic Nerd World refugees that pass for members of the male sex at school. But it felt different this time, less like a game. Of course I couldn't be the first to crack. I wasn't going to give him that satisfaction. But holding on felt like I was committing myself to something, and the longer I held on, the deeper I was being pulled in . . .

Thank God for grans and interruptions.

'She'll be out with her new pals.' I got a horrid flash of Mum, sitting by the phone in her old towelling dressing-gown, waiting for it to ring. But she wouldn't be on her own, she didn't know *how* to be, she was probably practising primal screaming with the gang right this minute. 'I'll try later.'

'Milly's parents are newly divorced,' Gran told Dominic. 'It's been a rotten year for her.'

'It has *not*!' When had I *ever* asked anybody to make allowances? 'And they're not divorced yet, it's not final.' How pathetic that sounded. Crazy as it was, I was still clinging to the hope that I could somehow stop my universe from disappearing down some guzzling, cosmic plughole.

'My parents never bothered to get married,' said Dominic.

'Ah,' said Gran. 'You're a love-child.'

He grinned.

'Whatever that means,' he said.

'Oh, there were a few slip ups in my day too. I had a school friend, who . . . Were you adopted?'

'Fostered. They've been OK, mind. I've had things my real mother could never have give me.'

'Like university.'

'Yeah.' His eyes flicked towards mine. 'Like university.'

Gran was silent for a moment.

'Does she know you're coming?' she said softly. 'It's your mother's face you're chasing, isn't it?'

He looked away, still smiling, his thick fingers probing his shirt pocket for his tobacco tin. The sunlight shifted in his pale hair.

'You won't be too hard on her, will you?'

'Hey!' He flicked open the tin. 'I'm not going to pick any fights. I'm curious, that's all, I don't blame her, she were only a kid. Milly's age. It's easier for girls now.'

'Do you remember her?'

He shook his head, moistening the edge of a cigarette paper with his tongue.

'I've got this picture, you know, in my head. But it's not a memory. It's just what you make up for yourself.'

'You ought to telephone,' said Gran. 'The shock . . . it might make things . . . it's just my opinion you know.'

He lit up.

'You don't have to worry about me, Emmy.' Why did I *hate* it so much when he called her that? 'It's nice to have somebody to worry, mind. You can be my foster-gran.'

'D'you think we should be making a move?' You can imagine how sorry I was to interrupt this cosy little bonding session. 'I mean, since nobody wants a sandwich.'

'There's nothing to stop *you* eating them,' said Gran.

'Bubble-wrap and fishpaste? No, thank you.'

'I just hope you never find out what it's like to be really hungry.' What was she *playing* at? Treating me like some little kid, putting me down in front of Dominic. She didn't want him to like me, that's what it was, she didn't want him to think I had any opinions worth listening to.

'Why don't you tell us about your friend?' I said. 'It's the first *I've* heard about it. I thought everybody was supposed to be so moral in your day.'

'She was taken advantage of,' said Gran levelly.

'Oh, come on! Nobody has to be taken advantage of!'

'He was older than her.'

'So why didn't she take him for all she could get?' I knew *somebody* who would've done, a cheap little tart, a family-wrecker, a grave-robbing bimbo . . .

'Milly, she was *your* age! Women were at the mercy of the men in those days. There was no DNA testing, no benefits, no council flats—'

'Well, it's horrible! An old man and a young kid—it's vile, it's sick!' I got up, jolting the table. Tea slopped over the bubble-wrap sandwiches.

'There's that poltergeist again,' said Gran.

'Oh, shut up!' I screamed at her. 'Just—*shut up*!'

And bolted back to the Ladies.

I couldn't believe what I'd done. And in front of Dominic. But I couldn't believe Gran either. It was just so *unlike* her.

'You OK?' said a quiet voice.

'You can't come in here!'

He rested his hand on the wall above my head, trapping me against the sink.

'Are you pregnant?' he said. 'Is that it?'

Any other question and I could have kept up the pretence. But he was so absurdly and staggeringly wide of the mark that my guard went completely. I started to laugh, and my face crumpled like a can crushed in somebody's fist, and everything I'd been trying to hide ran out, salty and noisy and ugly and obscene.

'Pregnant? It's not *me* who's pregnant!' I clawed the slime off my face. It was like dragging off some disgusting, dissolving latex mask that I'd been wearing— for how long? More than a year now. And it had finally self-destructed. 'It's not *me* who's pregnant—it's *Dad*!'

15

'Oh, Dominic, it was *awful*! The *look* on their faces.
They were so *pleased* with themselves—'
'Hang on, hang on. Who was?'
I twisted away from him, and clung on to the basin.
'Dad and Sherry—Sherrylynne . . . ' My teeth were
chattering. I caught sight of my face, unruly with grief,
mouth all over the place, a real horrorshow. 'They were
supposed to be having supper with us and then taking me
to see this band. Sherry's his girlfriend, but I never took
her *seriously*, she just wasn't a contender, I mean she's not
much older than *me*. And Mum and Dad were laughing
and joking, getting on so well. I honestly thought they
were starting to realize—'
'Realize what?' He touched my shoulder. I should have
been numb to everything except my own agony and
despair, but it was as if he'd burned his fingerprints into
me.
'What a *mistake* it all was. All the girls at school said
when it's over it's over, but I didn't believe them. I told
myself: so long as we keep calm, so long as we don't do
anything to make Dad run away even faster . . . '
'And what happened?'
'They just came out with it. *We're getting married.* Soon
as the final bit of paper comes through. And Mum just
stood there, like he'd hit her with a brick. And then she
looked at Sherrylynne and she said, ''Is it what I think it
is?'' And Sherrylynne went all coy and simpery and
said, ''Yes,'' and stuck out her skinny belly to show us—'

81

I felt fresh tears erupting. Dominic's hand moved up to my neck. His rough, swollen fingers massaged the nape, sending hot shivers all through my body, like scalding sand poured between the shoulder-blades. 'I thought, for one mad moment, Dad was going to say it was all a joke.' I turned to face him, because that's what his fingers were telling me to do. 'And then he put his arm round her, and he looked so—*proud*. That's what really hurt. And then Mum lost it, like she does, and he said, "I'm not getting into this," and they walked out, and I said such *horrible* things to Mum, and I told Gran a whole bunch of lies, and I *hate* him, Dominic, I hate him, I hate him, I *hate* him.'

He reached out and wiped the tears off my face with his thumb. He licked his thumb. His eyes smiled into mine. And the crazy thing was, I didn't even like him, I didn't trust him, he was exactly the kind of guy Dad would have been horrified to think I had anything to do with, and yet a part of me was craving him in the most abject, awful way, craving his approval, just because he was a man, because he was bigger and older than me and because nobody else approved any more, because I'd lost whatever it was that made them—men—Dad—approve of me.

'Keep very still . . . '

His face moved towards mine. *He's going to kiss me*, I thought wildly. What do I do? Do I keep my eyes open, or what? I mean, sex education's all very well, but they don't teach you a thing about *technique*. I shut my eyes. I felt the heat from his skin, closer and closer, then a cool movement of air that smelled of nicotine and gum. What was he doing? *Blowing* on me? My knees wobbled.

'That's it,' he said. I opened my eyes. 'You had a wasp on your hair. It's gone now.'

'Oh.' A black hole of disappointment opened inside me.

'Will you be OK?'

'Yeah. Sure. I just need a minute on my own.'

I checked myself in the mirror. No wonder he hadn't kissed me. My eyes were like thumbnail marks in pink pastry. I couldn't breathe through my nose, couldn't even blow it, it was as hard as a toffee. I soaked a big wodge of paper towels in cold water and held it against my cheeks. I still looked like an angry baby with a bad hangover. My head was banging and my teeth felt like felt.

He was leaning on the wall outside, smoking.

'Here.' He gave me his sunglasses.

'You won't say anything to Gran, will you?' I croaked.

'No.'

We started walking. He didn't try to touch me, and I was sorry and glad. The awful relief of having finally blabbed it all out was already giving way to a wariness, an unease. I was in his debt now. He'd got something over me.

'I pity Dad, that's all.' I couldn't have him thinking I was just some dumb kid who couldn't handle something as ordinary and banal as her parents splitting up. 'How could he let her trap him like that? The oldest trick in the book.'

'You're an only child, aren't you?'

'*What?*' I could have hit him. 'Are you saying I'm *spoiled*? It's not *me*, it's *Mum*. She can't cope. This last year's been so—I just can't do it any more.'

'Parents are only temporary.' He blew out smoke. 'You live with them, you move on. You'll be in college before you know where you are.'

'Oh, sure. If there's any money left to pay for me, if they don't want it all for the brat.' I couldn't believe I could have such ugly, greedy instincts. But I'd said it now. It was real.

'You might have a brat of your own,' he said, his tone unexpectedly brutal.

'What kind of loser do you think I am?'

'I've got a kid.'

Why did I find that so shocking? After all, he must have been twenty-two, twenty-three. I felt worse than shocked. I felt cheated, somehow. I was glad he couldn't see my eyes.

'We were just kids ourselves. Her mam wanted her to have an abortion. Said I were worthless. I don't see them any more. She went off me. I just send the money.'

'That's big of you.'

He shrugged. 'She got what she wanted.'

'Isn't that what you're supposed to say about the man?'

'It weren't up to me.' He flicked his cigarette away. 'She's happy enough. She likes to go on telly, you know, morning chat-shows. Been on a couple.'

'And what if, one day, your kid—'

'Jimmy. He's a little boy.'

'Jimmy, sorry.'

'I used to have a picture of him, to show people, like. But he'll have changed that much . . . I don't suppose I'd recognize him now.'

'And what if one day Jimmy comes looking for you? Don't tell me you'd run away! If you really believe all that stuff about parents being temporary, how come you're chasing round the country after a face you don't even remember?'

'Oh, that. I lied.'

'Well, that's really pathetic.'

'Summat to say in the car. People expect a bit of a life-story.'

'We told you the truth!'

'Hi!' Gran was coming to find us. 'Everything all right?'

'Meet you in White Burn Sands tomorrow, two o'clock.'

He spoke low and rapidly. 'On the marina by the Mermaid's Tail.'

'In a parallel universe!'

'I like the specs!' said Gran.

I snatched them off and shoved them at Dominic. He put them on.

'Still warm,' he murmured in the same private voice. I felt hot and sick inside, with anger and a strange excitement.

16

I could feel them moseying along behind me, taking forever. Gran was nattering away happily. She thought he was a poor lost child looking for his mum, not somebody's absentee father. I was glad he'd told me about Jimmy. It had put me right off him. There'd been a moment back there, when I'd come close to forgetting what this trip was all about.

And he had the cheek to call me spoiled! Was it *my* fault I was an only child? Was it *my* fault I'd taken it for granted they could never love anybody more than they loved me? And now Dad was in love with somebody young enough to be in the netball team, and she was going to produce some disgusting little sprog, and there wouldn't be enough money for me to go to university, and I wasn't going to be the person I was supposed to be any more. Wouldn't *you* be angry? Wouldn't *you* want to kill someone? Spoiled? I'd been spoiled all right.

Emmy was lucky. They were better people then. Not temporary parents, toys you have to give back at the end of the afternoon.

I'd have let him see his kid . . .

Yuck and double yuck!

I don't even *like* kids.

I waited by the car while they came strolling up together. He looked so protective, slowing his stride so she wouldn't have to hurry, leaning towards her to show that he was listening. Scumbag.

I thought of a name for Dad's new baby. The Big Zit.

Because it was the last thing in the world you'd want popping out.

'Something's made you smile!' said Gran, taking out her keys. 'Here.' She gave them to Dominic. How had he wangled *that*? 'I'll go in the back this time. You young people can sit together. You'll have much more to talk about.'

Dominic drove with great dash and verve, elbow out of the window, fingers thrumming to the heavy metal in his head. We raced above bristling brown moorlands that were frizzled up and smoking like old scorched doormats. A sign sailed past: *Newcastle 55 miles*. Already! We didn't speak. I didn't know what to say. I was inhibited by the nearness of him, by the smell and the heat coming off him. And I was fascinated. By the possibility of him. As if I had somehow embarked on a different journey from the one we were on already.

'So many families nowadays are part-time,' remarked Gran. 'Half the girls in Milly's class come from broken homes. It's a good school too. Oh—that sounds awful! Milly, rescue me!'

'Simple evolution.' I tried to sound cynical and old. 'None of my generation will get married. It'll be just an amusing old custom, a footnote in the history books.' As if we didn't spend all our dinner hours gazing at wedding displays. The walking wounded, window-shopping for weapons of mass destruction. 'We'll be able to get a baby out of a packet. Just add water.'

Oh, God. School. Shannon and Tori. I couldn't bear it. Ending up just the same as everybody else. Next year was supposed to be *my* year. My GCSE year. Everything had to be perfect. How could it be if I was on shitty nappy duty every time I went for my Quality Time with Dad?

I'd be better off in the park with a buggy of my own. Funny. I used to see them all there sometimes—the Moo Cows—and feel so superior. Me and my Great Expectations. Now I wasn't so sure. It was like they'd finally found an exam they could pass, and it was a subject I didn't know the first thing about.

'You can't get divorced from your kids.' That's what Leanne Roberts said, when they asked her why she wanted to keep her baby.

Oh, yes, you could. If you were Dad.

Was it because I stopped being cute? Is that why you stopped loving me? Did I make you feel old? Is that why you ran away?

Then don't you *dare* tell me to grow up.

Because I might just do it.

'Sly cake!' said Gran unexpectedly from the back.

'What's that when it's washed?' laughed Dominic.

'It was what the bakers made out of their old stale buns, all mashed up together and re-cooked. I just got a taste of it, now, after all these years—isn't that odd? A cheap treat. Mother knew all the angles. Cracked eggs were cheap too. And tripe, of course. "Purl or plain?" The butcher made that same joke every time we went in. And it still tasted like old vests.'

'Wasn't there *anything* nice?' I asked.

'Oh, there was a lovely chip shop just down the street! For a farthing, you could get a bagful of the crunchy, battery bits they skimmed off the boiling fat.'

'Yuck!'

'And the smell from the pork butcher's—Heaven! He used to boil up the carcasses in big tubs behind the shop—'

'Oh, pur-*leeze*!'

'I knew you wouldn't like it! He used to stay open until after the second house at the pictures. You could get a hot pork sandwich for threepence, or a penny dip. That was a bit of onion in a bread roll, stuck on a fork and dipped in the liquor he'd boiled the pigs in—'

'Stop it! Stop the car! Let me out!'

'Honestly, you're so squeamish! You wouldn't have lasted five minutes in my day. *You* wouldn't be so fussy, would you, Dominic?'

'I'll eat anything, me.' Crawler. 'Mind if I smoke, Em?'

'No, no. All the men smoked . . . You know what I always fancied and never got? *Candied peel.* Mr Perks the grocer had a whole lemon and a whole orange crystallized in sugar in the window of his shop. He used to shave off tiny wisps with a very sharp knife for women to put in their cakes . . . '

I looked in the glove compartment for something very sharp to stab into Dominic's leg. No such luck. I wanted him to know that *I* wasn't prepared to put up with his second-lung smoke. I knew he was waiting for me to say something, so I just rolled him a ciggie, dead casual. The gummed edge of the paper stung my tongue and I thought I tasted blood, but I didn't make too bad a job of it.

'Light it for me, will you?'

'Sorry. I *don't* smoke. If I can avoid it.'

He grinned and put out a hand. I fitted the ciggie between his fingers and he put it into his mouth. I held up the lighter. The flame was shaking. That's because we were going so fast.

'Thanks.'

I turned away, tasting smoke he had just tasted.

'You didn't like him, did you?' said Gran.

'Coast Road!' I'd reached that stage of tiredness where I was reading things out like a little kid. 'Salt-Marshes,

89

two miles! I didn't like him driving, that's all. Kwik-Save! Photo-processing! Rock Novelties!'

The gorgeous blues of the afternoon were fading and failing. Street lamps and strings of seaside lights were coming on all around us.

'It's washing-up time,' said Gran.

'Eh?'

'Washing—thingummy—*lighting*-up time.'

'LOOK OUT!'

Gran stamped on the brakes, and the teenage girl who'd run out right in front of us, unfroze, giggling madly, and bounded on to the other pavement.

'You stupid, *stupid*—' Gran thumped the steering-wheel. 'You could have been—Shoot her, Milly!'

'What?'

'Shoo—*Shout* at her, Milly.'

'She's gone now.'

'I thought it was Wendy. I thought I'd killed her. Why are you children so . . . so . . . wossname?' Gran started up again.

'Who's Wendy? Why are we turning off here?'

'Ghost house,' said Gran.

'What?'

'*Guest* house. It's a *guest* house. We have to sleep somewhere.'

'But we're nearly there! Can't we find somewhere central?'

'I've waited over half a century. I can hold on one more night.'

'This is very difficult to eat!' Gran smacked at the straggling threads of chewing-gummy cheese connecting her mouth to the wobbly triangle of ham-and-pineapple. 'They should make concessions for people with temporary teeth. Glorified cheese on toast, this is, only the cheese is nasty.'

'Have some soup.'

'What's it supposed to be?'

'Pea and ham.'

'Could have fooled me.'

Don't ask me why we were eating takeaway and watching a load of fat Americans yelling at each other and having make-overs, when White Burn Sands was just a couple of miles down the road, because it wasn't *my* idea, OK?

I poked at the soup with my spoon. It was murky green with little rubbery bits of pink in it, like the stuff that drops out of old hot water bottles.

'Fancy a coffee, Gran?'

'My system's had enough of a punishing already, thank you. The stuff I've had to digest today.'

'You've hardly eaten a thing.'

'If *you* want one, don't let me stop you.'

'I *don't* want one.'

This was turning into one of those pointless arguments that I was more used to having with Mum.

'Hey! What about fish and chips? The crunchy, battery bits, remember? I could nip out and get some! I might even find the street where—'

'You're not going anywhere.' *What?* Since when did Gran give me *orders*? 'I won't have it, Milly. You brought me here, against my better judgement, you owe it to me to stay.' She saw the look on my face. 'I'm sorry, I'm sorry. I don't know what's got into me. I'm a bit scared, that's all . . . you know . . . that it won't happen.'

'It'll happen, Gran. We're both whacked, that's all.' I binned the pizza. 'By the way, is there a place here called the Mermaid's Tail?'

I don't know why I said it. I had absolutely no

91

intention of going, you understand. I just wanted to feel the name in my mouth, to hear what it sounded like in my voice.

'It's up the coast a bit. A big rock split in two . . . supposed to look like the tip of a fish's tail. Why d'you ask about that? Because of Wendy?'

'Wendy? Isn't that what you called that girl? The one who ran out into the road . . . ?'

'Did I? I don't know why. She just triggered something . . . '

'Aha! A mystery! Come on, Gran!'

'Oh, it was just one of those small town tragedies.'

'You've started, so you'll finish!'

'You weren't very sympathetic when I mentioned her before.'

'Oh . . . this is the girl who got taken advantage of, right? By the older man?' I wasn't sure I wanted to hear it now.

Gran nodded.

'Uncle Archie. He wasn't, of course. He was a friend of the family. A funny, fat, little man. I don't know how he persuaded her to go off with him. The police found them together down by the Mermaid's Tail. Mother hid the newspapers to protect me, but everybody knew. The women all said they'd seen it coming because she got her bosoms early, which was supposed to be a sign of low intelligence. She was only fifteen. They sent him to prison.'

'What happened to Wendy?'

'Mental home.'

'*What?*'

'It's what they did in those days. They could put you in just for talking back to your parents. Mentally defective, they called it.'

Unbelievable. In nineteen-thirty-wotsit, a fifteen year

92

old gets banged up because she's been molested by some perv old enough to be her father—and sixty-something years later, a teenage bimbo can just walk off with somebody else's dad. And that's *progress*?

'When did she get out?'

'I don't know, darling. Mother said it was best not to dwell on it. I haven't thought about her in a long time.'

So why remember *now*? Why did that memory, of all memories, have to come rushing out of the twilight and hurl itself under our wheels?

Was it a warning?

17

It was light again and I could hear somebody breathing in and out very calmly and gently. The tide had come in. I knew, with absolute certainty, that if I looked out of the window, I would see Dominic, walking along the beach in a long, black overcoat that lifted and flapped behind him like a rebellious shadow. The sand would be firm and dark, like wet cardboard, and he'd look up, and our eyes would meet . . .

I crept out of bed and checked myself in the mirror. I pushed my hair behind my ears. I clawed it interestingly round my face. I scragged it back behind my ears. I lifted a corner of the blind and stood well back.

Mist everywhere. As if every pot and kettle in the world had boiled dry. I could just make out a scenic view of wheelie-bins below and a bit of a garage wall.

Men!

I went back to bed.

When I woke up again it was twelve o'clock! Gran was still sleeping. Knackered, poor thing. I got dressed and went downstairs to scrounge us some brunch: orange juice, coffee, Scrabbled eggs (Mum's word for them because we always have them during late-night Scrabble sessions), the papers, and a carnation nicked off one of the tables in the dining-room.

'Oh, you angel!' Gran was awake. 'Pass us my pills, would you, pet? In my handbag. Two green, a white, and a red.'

'What are they all for?'

'They keep me going. Thanks.' She swallowed the first two and took a sip of juice. 'Yuck! What's this?'

'Freshly squeezed orange-juice.'

'Could have fooled me. They boil it, you know.' Gran picked up a piece of toast, scowled at it, and put it down again. 'Why do they have to swamp everything with butter? Probably not even butter. Probably that disgusting rape seed oil. They used to make lino out of it. They've destroyed the British countryside with that stuff. A green and pleasant land it used to be.'

'There's nothing wrong with rape seed oil.' I caught sight of two strangers in the mirror: a grouchy old woman and a sulky teenager. How had *they* got here?

'Don't let's quarrel, Gran. It's a fabulous day.' The sun had burned off the mist and it was already scorching outside.

'Just as well. It's a long drive back.'

'We can't see everything and get back today!'

'We'll set out as soon as you've finished your breakfast.'

'*What?*'

'We should never have come. Dragging me back here . . . '

'You loved it here! It was all you ever wanted—'

'I never had *anything* I wanted! You think it was all so perfect? You don't understand a thing!'

'Gran, what's the—?'

'*Don't touch me!*'

I stared at her in horror. Did *I* do this? Did *I* turn her into this crotchety old crone with the eyes of a terrified child peeping out through hers? What was *happening?*

'This is just a game to you, isn't it? Another little puzzle to solve, marks out of ten for your essay next term. It was my life, Milly—*my life!*'

I just stood there, feeling as if all my skin had been

blow-torched off. I can't handle it when people get angry with me. I just seize up.

'It was cruel of you, Milly. I never knew you had a cruel streak. I thought it had passed you by.'

'I wasn't being cruel! I wanted to *help*.'

'You wanted what *you* wanted, and to Hell with everybody else!'

'So I'm selfish as well as cruel?' I was going to cry, and I wasn't about to let her see me do that. I snatched up my bag. 'I'm sorry you hated the journey, I'm sorry you hated the food, I'm sorry you hate *me*. But I shouldn't be surprised. Everybody else does!'

'Where are you going?'

'What do *you* care?'

This time I didn't wait for an answer.

I didn't set out to do anything bad. It was just, like, everything was already so wrong, there wasn't any other direction I could take. I knew I shouldn't have gone shouting and banging out, but how could I let her just pack up and leave, without finding Elizabeth Whately's face? All I'd wanted to do was give her back her memories. Nobody respected me, they all treated me like I was some kind of disappointment. I'd wasted a huge chunk of my life trying to keep things together, trying to hold time still, and they'd all just gone marching on without me. Even Mum. OK, she'd thrown a wobbler when Dad and Sherrylynne dropped their little bombshell on Friday night, but that's just Mum. The truth was, after months of weeping, she'd wept herself new. Maybe she was glad that it was finished good and proper. A bit sorry for Dad, even.

Well, I wasn't up for that. *Dead Dad, dead Dad, dead Dad*. I stoked up my anger. *Deadly Daddy, deadly Daddy, deadly Dad.* How could you pick a girl with a name like *Sherrylynne*? How could you even *think* of *marrying* her? A *nineteen* year old? She ought to be in college instead of wrecking my chances of ever getting there. Serve you right if I do something to remind you just how old and stupid you really are.

I turned a corner, and there he was, coming towards me out of the fairground din, with his long-legged slouching amble and his self-mocking, Milly-mocking grin, and his shoulders half-hunched and his pale hair flopping. He was wearing a sleeveless white T-shirt. I was dazed by muscles, and veins lying on the surface of muscles. He had a leather jacket slung over his shoulder and a six-pack dangling from his fist.

'You're early,' he said. And stood there, smiling.

'I thought you were in Newcastle.'

'Oh, aye? So you just happened to be taking a stroll and you just happened to find the Mermaid's Tail?'

He pointed to a sign above my head. A lady with a fishy tail and a big pink chest. I hadn't come looking for it, I swear I hadn't. I didn't know it was a pub he meant.

'Gave the old girl the slip, then?'

'She's not an old girl!' I tried to sound stern, but my mouth insisted on smiling, my mouth didn't want to put him off. I was glad of my make-up. Something to hide behind.

'Want to see the fair?'

'Spinning teacups and varnished horses?' I tried not to sound keen. 'Not exactly Blackpool Pleasure Beach, is it?'

'Suit yourself. I'm going on the rifles.'

He was a dead shot.

'Are you impressed yet?' he asked, after his third go.

I made a face.

'Here,' said the stallholder, annoyed. 'Pick one of the cuddly toys for your girlfriend.'

97

'I'm *not* his girlfriend.' How uncool it sounded, like insisting that Mum and Dad weren't really divorced.

He picked out a fluorescent blue rabbit. It was so ugly I was almost sorry for it. He put it into my arms. I couldn't not protect it.

'We could pretend,' he said. 'Just for the day.'

I rubbed the rabbit's ear, and its blue fluff gave off small, sharp shocks of static electricity.

'Want a lager?' He broke off a tin from the pack and snapped the ring. Foam rushed up through the aperture and dripped over his thumb. He held out the can. I had a mad, wild urge to lick his hand.

'After you.'

He tipped back his head and took a long swallow. His Adam's apple moved up and down, jutting from the front of his throat like a spike. I couldn't take my eyes off it. He squared his head again and looked at me, wiping his mouth with the back of his hand, then the top of the can with his thumb. I took it, and drank, throwing back my head, taking the bitterness in. An invited darkness. Some of it got up my nose and I choked and snorted, my eyes watering. I took another swallow to prove I could do it.

'Here.' I pushed the tin back at him. His fingers closed round my fingers.

'Now, then,' he said. We looked at each other. As if a bargain had been struck. How Dad would *hate* you, I thought. And the joy was fierce and frightening in me.

'When does she want you back?' His voice was rough, stroking. His thumb rubbed the outside of my thumb.

'Not too late.' My own voice squeaked like a fingernail on a blackboard. Pathetic. 'She's in a funny mood. I don't want to leave her too long . . . '

He let go. Took a last swallow and crumpled the can. Looked around, as if trying to make up his mind.

'It's not me,' I said. 'It's Elizabeth Whately.'

'Who?'

'I've got to find her face. For Gran.' But it wasn't for Gran. I did it to stop him going. I told him everything. All her private stuff. Everything I hadn't wanted Gran to tell him.

'All right,' he said. 'We'll check it out.'

'You don't mind?'

'Nah. Be interesting. I like the old girl.'

I was off the hook again. I wasn't just a tangled bunch of nerve-endings sparking and fizzing with a dark desire for revenge. I was on a mission.

But I was still fascinated by him, fascinated and afraid. Like the first time I was up close to a horse. The bigness of him, the grown-upness, the smell, something in the eyes. I was on my own with a full-grown, hairy, scary man! Tori and Shannon would be so *green*! He was everything we despised, and that gave him status. A bit of rough. 'So, how were your holidays, Mill?' 'Oh, you know. Dad's got his girlfr—Dad's girlfriend's gone and got herself pregnant, silly Moo Cow, so he's promised to marry her, poor, sad sap. But never mind *them—guess what I* got up to . . . ' Dot, dot, dot.

That's the problem. The dot, dot, dot.

What do you actually *do* in the dot, dot, dot?

And do you have to?

Of course I didn't. I hadn't made any promises.

And I could get away any time.

18

'Fish skinned on request!' I was doing it again, the tripperish thing, reading stuff out loud. A mixture of nerves and exhilaration and lager. We stared in at the chippy window, where a cat sat, fat as a jar of Greek oil, with a black trickle of tail curled around its base. 'D'you think this is the one? Where she used to get her bits battered—I mean her battered bits!'

'We're not there yet.' Dominic had the map. 'These places could do with gutting and starting again.'

'But look at the lovely old tiling! And the bits of stained glass with the prop-pirate . . . the pop-eye-rate . . . the *owner's* name in it!'

'And I bet you do all your shopping in out of town supermarkets.'

He was right, of course. We never walked down streets as poky as this. We hardly ever walked.

'So? I'm time tripping! Any objections? Hang on— must get a picture—' CLICK! 'Gran'll just *love* this! Hey— a pet shop! Fat Balls!' I shrieked with excitement. 'Sows' Ears! And look at the baby rabbits! All curled up together like pairs of mittens . . . aaahhh . . . Kidney Stones!'

'Eh?'

'Whoops! Kandy Store! Gran did that yesterday, got the words all wrong. Are you dying to get me trunk? Drying to get me—Omigod—what's *that*?'

A white van like an ambulance. Back doors gaping. Things hanging up inside. Suits of flesh in a white wardrobe. Pink and white pyjama-striped carcasses.

'Fancy a hot pork sandwich?' grinned Dominic.

'Ugh! Oh, God—*look*!' A hooded man in white wellies and white overalls splashed with pink was disappearing down a passage between the shops with a netted torso over his shoulder. 'It's barbaric!'

'Emmy was right. You're too squeamish.'

'What d'you want me to do? Buy a yard of tripe as a souvenir? OW!'

'Might not be a bad idea. Will you stop falling off the pavement, please?' He offered me his arm. I took it gingerly and he pressed it against his side, trapping my fingers. I felt muscles against my knuckles, muscles against my palm. 'OK, Milly, deep breath. It's just round this corner.'

'What am I going to *tell* her?' I wanted to lie down in the street and climb into a bin liner and pull it over my head. 'An arcade! Fruit machines! It's just *gross*!'

'Let's take a couple of pictures anyway.'

'She won't want to see *this*! We don't even know which is the right bit. There must have been four or five shops here at least.'

'What number was it?'

'Ninety-seven. But what use—?'

'Count the upstairs windows. It's only the façade that's changed.' Dominic tipped back his head. 'Right. We know this one's eighty-five, so Whately's Wheels must have been . . .' His lips moved. His finger prodded the air. '. . . *that* one!'

'Which?' I lifted the camera.

'Where the woman is.'

CLICK!

In the trillionth of a second before my finger moved, I saw her. Exactly as she was in Gran's photograph. Big

101

cottage-loaf of hair. High-necked blouse with leg-of-mutton sleeves. Looking down into the street from her upstairs parlour.

I lowered the camera. The window was empty.

'Dominic . . . ' I felt giddy and a bit sick. 'What *exactly* did you see?'

'Up there? Just some woman. What's the matter?'

'I think . . . I just saw Elizabeth Whately . . . don't ask me how. That was her special window.'

He looked at me.

'It *was* her! That was her window! I can't just walk away. I'm going up there to find out!'

I marched into the arcade.

'Is there a way upstairs?' The cashier stared at me. 'Upstairs. I want to go upstairs.'

'It's not allowed.' She was feeling under the counter for the panic button.

'Not even for a minute?' Dominic came ambling up behind me. 'Just this once?'

She took her finger off the button.

'It's just offices,' she said, flicking her hair. She had very blonde hair. And a black see-through blouse with a tacky black bra underneath it. 'Store rooms and that. It's not allowed. I'm sorry.'

'Sure, no problem.' He was doing his smiley thing on her. It was working too. It was horrible to watch, it was so obvious. 'Worth a try, though, eh? You see Milly's family used to live here, and we just . . . but it doesn't matter.'

'Well . . . ' She flicked some more hair. 'Maybe just for a—Sorry. Supervisor's coming. No can do.'

'Forget it, then,' I snapped. 'Come on, Dominic.' He was practically over the counter and licking her face. Honestly. All a girl has to do is throw her hair around, and their brains turn to frogspawn. 'Dominic?'

'What's your problem?' He grinned, following me out.

'It's not me who's got the problem,' I said, flicking my hair. I wanted him to look at me the way he'd looked at that fat slapper. The way Dad looks at Sherrylynne . . . 'Just tell me where we can get these developed.'

'There's a photo-lab at the end of the road. The old church. You'll get them back in an hour.'

I glanced up at the window. I was already losing faith in the idea. After all, why would Elizabeth Whately be wearing clothes she wore before Emmy was born? Answer: because that was the only picture of her I'd ever seen, that's why.

'So how do we fill up an hour?'

He smiled.

'I'll think of something,' he said.

'Dominic—NO! STOP! You mustn't! Stop it! STOP!'

People were turning to look. Their faces rushed past, like pictures in a book flipped through fast. Outraged, astonished, envious. I opened my mouth and let out a long, sweet scream of delight.

He slowed to walking pace.

'Let me out of this wheelchair, Dominic. *Now*. Let me *out*.'

'You sat in it.'

'I didn't ask you to kidnap me! There's probably some poor old geezer just doddered out of the loo, wondering where it is!'

'Now, now, don't make a scene,' Dominic put on a prissy, nursey voice. A middle-aged couple were strolling towards us, eating ice-cream wafers. 'It'll be tears before bedtime.'

'I'm not *kidding*, Dominic.'

'She doesn't get out much,' Dominic told the woman in a tone of breezy confidentiality. 'It's tragic, really.'

They stopped and looked.

'She's very brave,' said the woman. 'Isn't she, George?'

The man stared at me. His ice-cream was dissolving, slipping out from between the two soggy bits of biscuit. He licked the side of his hand, chasing the melted ice-cream up his wrist.

'What's wrong with her?' he said.

'It's an inherited thing. It only affects the females.'

'Is that right?' said the woman.

'Oh, aye! At the age of fifteen . . . ' Dominic accelerated. ' . . . they all . . . turn . . . into . . . mermaids!'

He ran to the end of the prom and tipped me out onto the beach like sand from a barrow. I rolled over and lay on my back. The sunlight was sweet on my skin, the salty air clean in my mouth. He stood over me, digging a booted foot in on either side. I smiled, and felt the heat on my teeth.

'You know what you are?' I said, studying him through squidged eyelids. 'You're the boy I was never allowed to play with. Who chased the girls with a jellyfish and made them cry.' I flipped over on to my stomach and tried to wriggle away. He put a foot on my shoulders, pinning me down, not hard enough to hurt. I felt powerless and powerful. Sexy, dangerous, helpless, guiltless. The best I'd felt all year.

'I want an ice-cream,' I said. 'Get me an ice-cream.'

He lifted his boot. I leaned my cheek on my bare arms, enjoying the smell of my own skin, and watched his long, denim legs scissoring over the sand. I liked this game.

He brought me an obscene-looking dollop of something, all squirmicellied with different coloured sauces. I sucked its cold sweetness greedily up out of the cone. I hadn't realized I was so thirsty.

'I want to paddle!'

I stood up, smacking sand off my bum with my free hand. A row of ancient mermaids in wheelchairs and quilted legbags smiled at me, nodding their approval. I was beautiful to them, just because I was young. It was good to be young. I'd forgotten. I kicked off my trainers and rolled up the bottoms of my jeans. I squeezed the warm grittiness up between my toes.

The sea was a way off, spread thinly, like the fresh surface sprayed on to an ice-rink. First the sand turned cool and sticky like fudge, then glossy and cold, stiffening all the tiny invisible hairs on my legs, fastening itself around my feet, making a soft lip-smacking sound each time it let me go. At the water's edge I dipped in a toe, and my tongue-tip deep into the cold flame of the cornet. The water was achingly cold, clasping my ankles, effervescing like Liver Salts. The ice cream gave me a faint pain between the eyes. I found stray sharpnesses beneath my instep and bits of grit with my probing tongue . . .

'You coming in, Dom?'

I looked round and he was pulling off his shirt. The effect was like sunstroke. The day seemed too hot, too bright, it was like a darkness descending. He was talking to someone, an enormous biker, sweltering in leathers, with a big, fat baby under his arm, as pink and juicy as a hot dog. I was going to call out when I saw something pass between them. Dominic tucked it into the pocket of his jeans. He was coming back. I turned away, and saw the wave rearing, pulling green-veined water up into itself like a muscle. I stepped back, dropping my ice-cream. The wave hung above me for a breathless moment, and teetered, and smashed itself into blossoms. The water pulled away, as if it were being dragged through a gigantic mangle. I felt the sand slither and suck under my feet, a queasy, uneasy sensation, like when a train moves off from the platform next to yours, and you don't know who's moving, you or it.

'You ready?'

He'd tied his shirt round his waist. I tried not to stare at his chest. He had a tattoo of a swallow on his left shoulder. I looked at that instead. That was just as bad.

'You want to take them off.' He pointed at the watersogged bottoms of my jeans.

'I'm OK.' I stumbled along beside him like a mermaid on dry land. 'I ought to be getting back anyway.'

'What's wrong? You think I'm going to attack you? Eh?' He was laughing.

'No.'

'What, then?' He stopped.

'Nothing.'

'Don't give me that.'

'All right. What did you get off that man?'

'What do *you* think?'

'I asked first.'

'You think I'm going to drug you? Is that it?'

'I didn't say that.' It felt stupid, horrible, having to justify myself.

'You don't have to come along, you know. It's nothing to me either way.'

'I just want you to *tell* me!'

He looked at me, his eyes mocking, thinking about it.

'OK.' He put his hand in his pocket.

'No—it's all right! I trust you, OK? I'm sorry, it wasn't my business.'

'I don't want you thinking—'

'I'm not. Wait!' I pulled off my jeans (my T-shirt was just long enough to cover my knickers) and rubbed my legs dry with the tingling, sandpapery sand. It was a bit like washing in fizzy pop. But my legs aren't bad, even if Gran

106

thinks they're too little. I could see that Dominic liked them anyway.

We walked the length of the trippers' beach, swinging the blue rabbit between us like our child, glugging lagers and sharing roll-ups. I hated the taste, but I wasn't going to make myself look even dumber than I already had, so I just sucked in the smoke and blew it straight out again. It's pretty yucky, the wetness from somebody else's mouth. Then there's this sudden burst of heat as the tobacco burns back towards you, like gunpowder rushing down a fuse, and the paper spits and sizzles. But there were girls watching and envying me, and it was worth it for that.

We stopped at a stall filled with rows of little pink crabs all with their arms folded like rugby players posing for a team photo. He bought me a tub of chewy things that tasted of the sea and not much else, and told me they were winkles and they came off the sewer pipes, and laughed when I spat them out in disgust.

Cliffs sprouted up, battlements of clay and chalk, dribbling brown liquids, cutting us off from the town. We walked on a lumpy white pavement like toothpaste gone hard, all strewn about with white boulders, as if an ogre had spent centuries crunching up and spitting out ogre-sized Mint Imperials. The sea glittered like a drawer full of clean knives, and there was all this black, fringed seaweed everywhere, like heaps of dead poodle skins. It popped slimily underfoot like dead bubble wrap.

And then the mist came down again, and the sea became a strange room with all its furniture covered with dustsheets, and all I could see were two wrinkles of water with brightness on them and nothing beyond, and I looked back, and Dominic wasn't there. The mist moved around me, like an animal, getting my scent. I was terrified at the thought of trying to pick my way back through the dead poodles and the Mint Imperials with the liquid gunge gurgling in between, and then a hand came out of the mist and I thought I'd explode with relief.

'*Dad!*'

I could feel the callouses on his palms, the bones in his fingers. The sheer size of his hand was thrilling. So safe, so dangerous. He put his leather jacket over my shoulders and tugged me towards him, and it was as if a door had opened in him and I had fallen into a dark and dizzying place.

And still he didn't kiss me. He was clever, you see. He had protected me, he had rescued me, he had made me break the rules, he had been my friend, my guide, my accomplice. Soon it would be my turn to do something for him.

He led me, stone-stepping over the Mint Imperials, to a staircase cut into the cliff. There was a rusty metal rail, and coils of dog poop squirted here and there. He kept hold of my hand as we climbed out into the sun.

'What's that?' I said, looking back and down at the mist moving away, and a long, dark rock emerging, split in two.

But I knew already.

'They call that the Mermaid's Tail,' he said.

I stroked my rabbit's blue, electrifying fur. It snagged my fingernails and made me shiver in the heat.

19

So here we were. Where I'd always known we had to end up. The three of us. Me, Dominic, and the bed.

'Honestly, it was puke-inducing!' I was telling him about what Dad had said on the phone, you know, the stuff I couldn't tell you before? 'He said she was the best thing that had ever happened to him, and she and I would simply *lurve* each other if I'd only give it a chance. She was his *temp*, Dominic, can you believe it? Poor, sad man! I mean, what *happens* to these guys? Do they wake up one morning and realize they've turned into a stereotype?'

He cracked open another can.

'I mean, how did she get pregnant in the first place? Nobody has to these days—sorry. I suppose you didn't get sex education in your school.'

'Not to GCSE standard.' He sprawled in his chair, his legs wide.

'What? Oh, right. Well, you must be exceptionally fertile—for a man today, I mean.' I was a bit drunk, a lot panicky. 'It's all these plastics in the food-chain. Men are only half as fertile as they were fifty years ago. Not the same men, of course. She did it on purpose, Dominic, she *targeted* him, a nice, middle-aged man who's already made his pile and won't dare stray because nobody else is ever going to fancy him.'

He shrugged. He did a lot of shrugging. I could read what I liked into it.

'Are you going to sit down?' he said.

'Thanks.' Frankly, I wanted to put down newspaper before I sat anywhere. The caravan smelled of mouldy carpet and old dogs' bottoms. There were unwashed plates around, empty cartons of take-away food. I sat on the edge of the bed with my bare knees nipped together, sipping my lager and hugging my blue rabbit. I told myself it wasn't too bad. I could leave at any time.

'What were your foster parents like?' I asked, to break the silence.

'Which ones?' He took another swallow.

'Oh. D'you still see any of them?'

'No reason.' He dried his smile with his fingers. I glimpsed cleaner skin under the ingrained dirt. He fitted one of his roll-ups into the smile. 'What I said before, though, that were true.' He flicked his lighter and squinted into the flame. 'I did go to look for my mother. Once.' He snapped the lighter shut and pocketed it, blowing out smoke. It hung and twisted in the sunlight above us, like a sheet flung up and settling over a half-made bed. 'She dumped me when I were three. But I never forgot her face. I knew her as soon as she opened the door.'

'Did she recognize you?'

'Oh, aye. She said: It's Matthew, isn't it?'

'But—'

'That's what she called me. I had different names, depending who fostered me.'

'Who called you Dominic?'

'Doesn't matter. Anyway, I'm standing there, grinning like an idiot. I can see inside. There's a kid playing a video game. A baby crying somewhere. And she's just stood there, waiting for me to go.'

'I'm sure she wasn't—'

'It were like she'd been hoping I'd be somebody famous. A pop star or an MP or summat. And I weren't. I weren't anything. I were just like her.' He laughed. 'All those years she'd been fantasizing about this secret son who were going to rescue her and change her life. And she saw it weren't going to happen. And she wished I hadn't come.'

'Oh, Dominic.'

'What d'you want? That's what she said. Nothing, I said. I were just passing. Oh, she said. Right, I said. See you, then. Yeah, she said.'

'That's just—awful.'

He shrugged.

'I got over it. I felt a bit like that kid in the story, the one who fights the pirates, and comes back and looks in the window and sees his mother with a new baby.'

'Peter Pan? If anyone's like Peter Pan, it's *Dad*. Trying to get back his lost youth by having a new baby.'

A spasm of irritation puckered his face. He didn't want to hear me bleating about Dad. We'd done that bit. But I *had* to keep on stoking my resentment, or I wouldn't be able to go through with it. And I owed him. More than ever now he'd told me his story.

'One good thing,' he said. 'I took summat away from her. I did that much.'

'What did you take?'

He smiled.

'Hope.' He took a last drag and dogged his cigarette. 'So that's where chasing faces gets you, little Milly. The way I'd remembered her were just summat I made up for myself. And she couldn't make herself into that person. She couldn't make herself glad to see me.' He finished his lager and crunched the can. 'So that were that.' We looked at each other. Gulls screeched in the air outside.

Fear crawled up from my stomach like a swarm of frozen wasps. I hugged the rabbit tighter. *Dead Dad, dead Dad, dead Dad.*

111

He stood up. All I could see was his chest, his arms.

'Is this your place?' I gabbled, to make him sit down again.

'Scotty's,' he said, stepping across the space between us. 'The guy on the beach. You don't need this, do you?' He took the rabbit from me and dropped it on to the floor. He sat down on the bed.

OK, OK. *Let's get it over with.*

He kissed like you'd kill to be kissed. He made my head swim and my heart bang and my knickers feel as if they were filled with tinsel. I was going under for the third time and the mermaids had hold of my feet and were pulling me down, down . . .

And suddenly, it all stopped. I don't know why. I could feel all the excitement running out of me and away like dirty water down the plughole, and the taste of him, beery and cigaretty, made my stomach heave.

'Wait—I'm not ready!' I tried to push him off, but his hands were underneath my shirt, so we were sort of knotted together. 'I'm not ready, Dominic!'

'It's all right,' he mumbled. 'I'll take care of that.' I didn't know what he meant. Then I did. I fought harder.

'Hey!' He grabbed my arms. 'What's going on? You were up for it a minute ago.'

'Well, I'm not now!' All the sexy feelings had evaporated. I tried to kick-start them, reminding myself how furious I was with Dad, but it just didn't seem a good enough reason any more. 'No! Please! I've changed my mind!'

'*I* haven't.'

'I'm sorry, I made a mistake, OK? Dominic—NO! I'm *serious*. Look—this is degrading, it's stupid, it's not fair on either of us—I don't even *like* you!'

'You don't have to like me.' His thumbs pinched into the muscles of my arms. 'Get real. You're not Daddy's little girl any more. Isn't that what you came here to prove?'

'No! I mean . . . *no*! I don't know!'

Yes I did. I wanted Dad to burst in, fists flying, come to rescue his Millybird.

'Please, Dominic.' This was serious humiliation time. 'Let me go. I'm only fifteen. It's against the law!' He laughed out loud. 'Please don't hurt me.' I was crying now, shameful, little-girl tears that melted all my make-up, washing off the face I had chosen so carefully for that day. 'Please don't hurt me.' But he'd already seen me cry. Been there, done that, got the merit badge.

'I can do anything I want,' he said. 'You know that. You knew that when you came looking for me.'

'Dominic, please let go of my arms—'

'I know what I am. I'm your dad's worst nightmare.'

'Dominic, let go—'

'That's why you came.' He shook me. 'Isn't it? Eh?'

'Dominic. please—'

'So you could spite the old man and it wouldn't be your fault?' He put his face close to mine. He had seriously awful teeth. 'Well, sorry to disappoint you. I'm not a child molester. But don't worry, there's plenty more out there if you really want to wreck your life.'

'Dominic, I'm going to be sick!'

He jumped aside, cursing, as it came splashing up, more shameful, more shocking than tears. The first spurt went all over my bare legs. It was warm, as well as knobbly. A bit like tripe. I got up. The room tilted and swerved.

'Here.' He pushed a towel at me. I stumbled to the door and finished the job in the bushes outside.

'You OK?'

I wiped my face. The towel was sour already. I wiped my knees. I was sober now.

'You'll be wanting these.' He dropped my jeans and carrier bag on to the grass, and stood in the doorway, looking at me with the same cynical, slightly amused expression that he'd been wearing the first time I saw him. 'Better have this, too.' He held out the rabbit by its ear. 'Go on, take it.'

'Dominic, I'm really—'

'Forget it. You want me to walk you back?'

'I'll be OK.'

'You sure?' He grinned. He really did need a good dentist. 'Of course, if you like . . . '

'What?'

'You could always come back inside and give it another crack . . . ?'

I looked at him through my snively, sicky hair.

'You loser,' I said. I threw the rabbit at him and ran.

20

My legs ached, my feet ached, my head ached. I felt as if somebody had lifted up my skin and swept a whole mess of grit and bits of broken glass underneath it. And then put it back and walked all over it. And I smelled horrible.

I wanted somebody to comfort me, to tell me it didn't matter. I wanted Mum and Dad.

I pushed open the door.

'Where've you *been*?' she screamed at me.

'Don't be cross, Gran—'

'You left me on my own! You *promised* you wouldn't leave me on my own!'

'I've been looking for your mother's face.' Too late, I remembered the film back at the photo-lab. Pictures of an empty window, an amusement arcade . . . 'Look!' I held out the carrier bag. 'I got you all this stuff—to show you nothing's changed and it's safe to go back! I've got sly cake! And candied peel—'

'Sly cake?' She dashed it out of my hand. 'Are you insane, or what? You think I want to be reminded of those times? The worst times in my life? They called this coast the poverty coast, did you know that?' Tears stood on her cheeks, tears of rage and exasperation. 'The taste of poverty, that's what sly cake was. They were terrible times, times nobody should ever have to go through. And you expect me to be glad it hasn't changed?' She looked so small, crunched up by her anger, like a fistful of brown paper; and I thought: what if this is the only face of Gran I

115

can ever remember, this furious, desperate face that *I* put there?

I was afraid to touch her. Even to take a step closer. I wanted it to stop, I wanted it to be a stranger, anybody, so long as it wasn't my gran this was happening to. I felt so helpless, worse even than that time with Mum, at least Mum didn't know I was there.

'I waited and *waited*.'

'Gran, don't.' I couldn't bear it. Didn't I say if Gran ever went to pieces we'd all had it?

'I woke up and you *still* weren't there. Nothing changes. I was always the one who mattered least. I tried not to mind, but I minded, *I minded*! And they still left me in the end! They *always* left me. So I made a family of my own, so it could never happen again, and you have to go and smash—' Appalled, I watched her double over, gasping for breath.

'Gran, are you all right?'

'Fetch me my spray. Spray! Handbag!'

That was something I could do. I grabbed her bag and tipped it out onto the bed.

'Is this it?'

She snatched the spray off me and squirted it into her mouth.

'Gran, what's happening? Is it asthma?' I never knew old people got asthma. But I never knew Gran was old until this weekend . . .

'It's all right. Don't fuss. I'll be fine in a moment.'

'D'you want me to fetch somebody?'

'NO! It's just the food. I told you the food's no good nowadays. I should have resisted it.' She sat, hugging herself inside her cardigan. She seemed sizes smaller than the day before.

'I'm sorry, Milly,' she said at last. 'I shouldn't blame

you. I've looked too far back and too deeply. I should have left things as they were.'

'It *is* my fault. I shouldn't have brought you here. I've just made things worse. I'm bad. I never thought I was, but I don't seem able to help it.'

'No, Milly. Darling. Come here.' I sank down on the floor and put my head on her lap. She stroked my hair. 'Milly, I've got to tell you something. Something I'm ashamed of.'

'No, *I've* got to tell *you*—'

'Please, Milly, let me do this. It's my own fault I've lost her face, and that's why I can't ever get it back.'

'But it was Mum who tore up the photo.'

'That's what I let you think. But it wasn't. I just wanted it to be her fault, I suppose.'

'*You* tore it up? *Why?*'

'It was when I first found out they were getting divorced. I was so angry with Joanna. So disappointed.'

'But you took it so *calmly*. I thought—'

'You think you're the only one who can put on a brave face?' I could hear the smile in her voice. Such a sad smile. 'It seemed as if she was just throwing everything away. Tearing up my whole life, making it meaningless. Perhaps I was punishing her . . . '

'By hurting yourself?'

'Don't you do that sometimes? Make things even worse for yourself when really you want to hurt somebody else?'

I didn't answer.

'One minute I was sitting writing my life story, and the next . . . I was so ashamed. I hid the evidence, and I hid my unhappiness away with it too. After all, it was no use to Joanna. And then, one night, in *you* march out of the blue and it all comes tumbling out together! And that's why I'll never get her face back. Because I don't deserve to.'

I wanted to confess, to confide, to give something in

117

return. I couldn't bear that she should think it was all her fault. That she could have told me something so hard to tell, while I was still hoarding secrets.

But I didn't want her to stop stroking my hair.

'You *were* happy, Gran. I could hear it in your voice when you were telling me your stories. It's just . . . well . . . happiness is always mixed up with a lot of other stuff . . . And he always came back, didn't he? So what did you mean about them all leaving you?'

'Want to know how it ends?'

'Yes, please,' I whispered, settling my head more deeply into her lap. 'Tell me the final chapter . . . '

*　　　*　　　*

It was the best summer ever, the summer she was Pop's Girl. He went to all her concerts, he read out her school reports at the table, he showed her off to his friends.

The reason for this rise in status?

Beryl had run off and got married. To somebody called Eddie Wallace. Father could never say the name without sounding as if it was stuck to his teeth and he was trying to spit it off. 'A jumped-up Johnny nobody knows anything about! Well, she'll not set foot in here again. I've still got *one* daughter left.'

Gus supplied all the details.

'They met in the Picture House Café. And they were seen holding hands in the chip shop. *And* he got thrown out of a dance hall for wiggling his hips—like this—and they're living with his parents at sixteen Birch Avenue. So bang goes your chance of being a bridesmaid.'

The night the news broke, Jack Whately stayed out very late. He got home minutes before Gus, who'd been bird's-nesting in the woods. He waited for the Son and Heir behind the door and gave him a thump that Emmy heard from her bedroom. Gus went roaring upstairs. It was the

118

first time Jack Whately had ever struck one of his children.

'You'll never hit me again!' shouted Gus from the landing.

And he was right.

The air cooled, the sea turned green as jellied eels, and an errand boy came whistling into the shop with a note for Elizabeth Whately. She put on her hat and gloves and went straight out. That evening she informed Jack Whately that Beryl was now his Extra Special Girl. He was going to be a grandad.

Coming up to Christmas, the weather was murderous. The wind walked the street armed with knives. It hurt just to breathe. Emmy grew chilblains as big as Brussels sprouts. It was agony trying to stuff her feet into her winter boots.

On the Saturday before Christmas, Olga from Sunday School's Uncle Larry brought his little boy into the shop. Olga's dad was a seaman who had been crippled in an accident abroad and was trapped in hospital there because they couldn't afford to bring him back. Her mother was a cleaner and they lived with Uncle Larry, his wife, and little Eric in the upstairs part of their grandmother's terraced house. The old lady lived downstairs and never went out. Emmy used to see her peeping from the window.

'I want the best you got!' Uncle Larry slapped his half-crown down on the counter. 'As many gears as you like!' He sauntered round, pinching a tyre here, setting a wheel whirling there. 'Made up your mind yet, lad?' Blushing with excitement, little Eric stammered that he would like the modest tricycle which Elizabeth Whately had wheeled out to show him.

'You'll be able to take it away the week after Christmas.' She entered the first instalment in the ledger.

'Champion!' Uncle Larry's eye followed the coin into

the till. 'Haway, man! Let's get on home and tell your mam.'

Elizabeth Whately watched them go up the street.

'I hope they can keep up the payments,' she said. 'Poor little lad.'

That same day, Jack Whately went shopping too, for a pair of pinstriped trousers and a frock coat. He'd been asked to stand as Tory candidate in the council elections and was tickled pink because he secretly voted Socialist.

'You'll never do it?' Elizabeth Whately was aghast.

'But *they* don't know that! I said I'd think it over! You see what it means, don't you, Lizzie? We're Somebody! And the whole town knows it! I'm invited to the Conservative Club tonight. I might look in.'

'I don't suppose they serve bees' wine?' asked his wife tartly. Bees' wine was what he drank when he was on the wagon. It only looked like beer.

'Don't be soft, woman. Drink's the only consolation a working man has.'

'You've got your wives.'

'And what choice did I have but learn to drink, the upbringing I had? A pub was somewhere to keep warm after I got away from the nuns. Blame them, the witches. It's thanks to them I've fallen away from the church.'

'So how come you were calling for a priest the other night, when you thought you were dying?'

'Well, you never got me one. Fine wife you are.'

'Well, you weren't dying, were you?'

Late that night, half-asleep, Emmy heard him tiptoeing heavily up the stairs and getting caught at the top.

'A drop of whisky for a chill! Would you deny me that?'

There were muffled negotiations, and stumbling footsteps along the landing to the spare room. She drifted back to sleep.

'Emmy, wake up.' It seemed just moments later. Beryl stood in the doorway. There was a calmness in her face that Emmy recognized from the Bad Old Times. 'Father's died in the night,' she said. 'We've laid him out in the parlour. You can come and look at him now.'

He was covered with a white sheet, turned back to show his face. Beryl had washed and shaved him, and combed his fierce black hair. Under the sheet, he lay naked on a board with a bucket beneath, 'to collect the bodily fluids'. The undertaker's men would dress him in his new frock coat and striped trousers and swathe him in purple for the benefit of visitors, but the real work had been done in the night by a young, pregnant girl.

'You have to touch him,' Mother said. 'Or you'll have nightmares.'

He was colder than it was possible to imagine. His face was still the furious red it had always been, as if he were on fire inside, fighting, fighting to get them to where he wanted them to be. His neck and chest were lily-white, the colour legs turn underwater. But he would not be surfacing again.

The doctor diagnosed pneumonia and a heart attack.

'Had he been drinking much?' he asked Elizabeth Whately.

'Only for a cold. He said it kept him going.'

'Any chest pains?'

'He had a bit of a cough. I heard him get up in the night. I should have gone to see . . .'

'I doubt there was anything you could have done.' The doctor signed the certificate and hurried out to his car. Business was brisk this cold snap.

Emmy bolted the shop door, and began taking down the Christmas decorations. She did not know what else to do. She carried them into the back room where they had their meals and she wrote her essays and Father did the accounts.

Someone was standing by Jack Whately's desk, with his shoulders hunched and his hat pulled down over his eyes . . . her father's overcoat and trilby, on the bentwood stand where he had left them.

Remembering how, when she was small, he used to let her slip her hand inside his glove with his own, she reached into the cold pocket of his overcoat and drew out a crumpled glove, like a hand. She put it on. What small hands he had had. They had seemed as big as a bear's. She took down his coat and held it for a moment. How small it was. The poor are always small. She hung it up again. Hanging up a life . . . He'd been just six years in the town.

Two days after Christmas, Uncle Larry's wife came round and cancelled the bike for little Eric.

'He'd no business getting us into debt,' she said angrily. 'Just to put a smile on the bairn's face.'

'Well, he had the anticipation, I suppose,' sighed Mother, after she'd gone.

Funny how things turn out. The secret wish Emmy had made all those years ago back in Newcastle came true at last. They say you should be careful what you wish for. Unable to stand the loneliness, Elizabeth Whately moved her things into Emmy's room. Gus took over the main bedroom.

'About time too,' said Beryl. 'He's growing up fast. And Ems will be married before we know where we are.'

'I'm not fourteen yet!' protested Emmy. She thought then that Beryl and her mother gave each other a look, and that Mother seemed fleetingly upset, but the moment passed.

Beryl and Eddie moved into a room on the top floor where Emmy and Gus had practised riding their bikes in wet weather.

'Don't worry, Mother. We'll make a go of this place.'

122

'Are we short of money?' asked Emmy.

'Not exactly,' said Elizabeth Whately. 'But we don't actually *own* anything.'

'There's not even the ten bob widow's pension,' said Beryl. 'Because he was self-employed.'

'We'll just have to put on a good front,' said Mother.

With newly-permed hair, new teeth, and a new coat, Elizabeth Whately went for a loan so that they could carry on the business. An enquiry agent came round to the shop. He had a little moustache and oil on his hair that came off on the backs of the chairs and he made eyes at Elizabeth Whately. I hope she doesn't marry him, thought Emmy.

That afternoon, Beryl took Emmy out and bought her a coral-coloured party dress with long, ruffled skirts.

'But it's *three pounds*! How can we possibly—?'

'You've never been to a school dance yet,' said Beryl. 'It's time you had a proper dress.'

She showed it off at home to the others.

'What a doll!' Eddie let out an appreciative whistle. Beryl gave him a look. 'Well, you know,' he amended. 'Nicer than that ugly old uniform, eh, Em?'

And Emmy understood at last.

'Am I not going back to school, then?'

'Of course you are,' said Mother. 'At least till you're fourteen anyway. After that, we'll see how you feel.'

Fourteen. Anybody could leave at fourteen, if they didn't want to do their School Certificate. Still, at least she had had the anticipation. Emmy held herself still and composed, trying not to let the beautiful, corrupting shell of the dress touch her. It felt just like coral is supposed to, stiff and sugar-sharp, as if she might cut herself on it, if she moved.

'We could do wonders with this place!' Beryl was saying. 'We've got all sorts of plans, you wait!'

Nobody noticed Emmy leave the room. She went upstairs and climbed carefully out of the crackling coral frock. She put on her ordinary clothes. Nobody heard her go out.

The woman in the shop wouldn't take it back.

'Well, I'll never wear it,' Emmy promised her bitterly.

Two days later, Mother opened a letter with the school crest on the top. A familiar, anxious line appeared between her eyebrows. She passed the letter to Beryl, who scanned it quickly.

'Later,' she said, in a low voice, glancing at Emmy.

Emmy found the letter by chance. She had to read it twice before she could take it in. They were offering her a free place so that she could stay on and get her School Certificate! She put the letter back where she had found it, and waited for the good news. Days passed, then weeks. Nobody said anything. By Easter, it was accepted that she was leaving. She dropped from third to thirteenth in the class. In her final report, the teachers expressed their disappointment that Emmeline had let her standards slip. What did *they* care? The whole thing had been nothing more than a cruel joke.

There was no fuss on her last day. Everyone was too busy in the shop. She put away her hockey stick and tennis racket in the back of the wardrobe and hung up her dress and blazer. Three summers ago, they had gone out and bought her a whole new life to grow into. It was just starting to fit. Now it was fit only for dusters.

She closed the bedroom door and wedged a chair under the knob. It was so long since she had allowed herself the luxury of tears, she didn't know if she could produce any. She sat down at the dressing-table and took off her glasses.

Why did you have to *die*? Everything I was going to do, everything I was going to be, was for *you*, to make *you* proud. And now I can't be or do any of it. Why didn't you come back? You *always* came back. And now, because you're not here to know or care, my life is to be crumpled up and thrown away.

Something was happening. A smarting sensation behind her eyes. She dropped her face into her hands and waited. A slow, single tear trickled over her wrist and down her forearm . . .

'Emmy? Can you give us a hand in the shop?'

She lifted her head, half smiling.

'With you in a minute!'

The tears would just have to wait a bit longer.

21

'Oh, Gran! Couldn't you have told them how you felt?'

'What for? I had to face facts. I was a grown-up now, part of the real world. French verbs are all very well, but they don't get the dinner cooked . . .'

* * *

'The baby's crying!' Eddie used to yell from the shop, and Emmy would run and see to it. There were two babies by now, three years had passed, and Emmy was seventeen.

Gus had been out of school a year. A local builder had offered to train him up, but he came home on the first day, filthy and frightened half to death. The other lads had thrown him in the lime-pit.

'You needn't go back,' said Elizabeth Whately. She bought him a motorbike and leathers to compensate, and opened an account for him at the Post Office. 'You'll get married,' she told Emmy, 'but a man needs money.'

Emmy didn't quite see the logic of that.

But Mother was full of surprises.

'Seen any nice houses today?' Beryl asked over supper one night. It was a standing joke that Elizabeth Whately liked to spend her afternoons looking at houses for sale.

'As a matter of fact, yes,' was the reply. 'So I put down twenty-five pounds as a deposit. There's no need to look as if you've been struck by lightning! It's too crowded here. Emmy and Gus can come in with me, and if you want to take over the business, Beryl, you can pay me three pounds a week.'

Beryl didn't need to think about it. Everyone wanted a bike with the latest fitness craze sweeping the country. And everyone knew Whately's Wheels. They even had their own advert showing at the picture house.

'Will they give you a mortgage though, Mother?' It was almost unheard of, a woman getting a mortgage, especially at Elizabeth Whately's age. But the bank reckoned they were a good risk. Things had changed a lot since that long distant day in court.

Privately, Emmy thought the risk too great.

Still, it was time for a change . . .

'And you'll still come over and mind the boys?' Beryl wanted to be sure.

'No,' said Emmy. And was surprised by the firmness in her voice. 'I want a proper job.'

'But we don't need you in the shop.'

'Then I'll find something else.'

'You'll be lucky!'

'A High School Girl?' smirked the clerk at the Labour Exchange. 'Well, I'm sure we can find something to suit. Let's see . . . They need packers at the salt works, there's a train leaves for the marshes at seven every morning. No? Like the films, do you? All the young girls do. There's a vacancy for a cleaner at the Empire. My, you *are* hard to please! That leaves the match factory or the grocer's in Bonaparte Terrace. Take your pick.'

There was a queue round the block for the job at the grocer's. Emmy got it because she'd been at school with the boss's niece. So her education had counted for something.

The grocer's was a big old shop run like a prison. The

127

manageress sat in a sort of fortress in the middle, doing the accounts. Everything followed a rigid routine. On Mondays, they scrubbed the wooden floors clean of all the bacon fat and biscuit crumbs from the previous week. On Tuesdays, the errand boys lugged in a great vat of butter, and the girls cut it into slices, wrapped each slice in greaseproof paper, weighed it and labelled it. Then they did the cheese, two kinds, cheddar and processed. The store closed at seven, and every surface had to be washed down and every knife scalded and polished before they could go home at eight. On Saturdays, they worked until nine. The shop door was always open, and the only heating was a gas ring in the back room where they had their tea. The errand boys used to rub the girls' hands for them. Their feet, too, sometimes. Emmy never permitted such liberties.

'You'll not grow rich on twelve and six a week,' said Beryl, miffed by this display of rebellion. Maybe not. But it was independence, of a sort.

Elizabeth Whately was like a young bride again in her new house, chasing the furniture with cloths like a bullfighter, smacking the dust out of the air. As soon as she had it the way she wanted, she invited Auntie Beattie to visit. Watching her hurrying round after Beattie with her eager, limping tread, Emmy began to understand what it was that her mother was trying to say with this big house, filled full of new furniture on the hire purchase. *Look, Beattie! I'm not the ailing little sister any more, the runt of the litter, the one who has to be baled out!* But she still looks like a little girl, thought Emmy, riven by an almost unbearable pang of affection, a little girl with grey hair and a bad leg, desperate for approval . . .

'No more blacking the grates!' Mother announced proudly, as Auntie Beattie inspected the kitchen with its tiled floor, dressers right up to the ceiling and brand new Aga with an enamel top. 'Isn't progress wonderful?'

'Nice white sinks,' conceded Aunt Beattie. 'I expect that lawn takes some mowing. I wonder you didn't buy something easier to manage. Is Augustus working yet?'

'Not yet.'

'Oh, well, you'll have him at home for a while anyway. Emmy's courting, I dare say?' Emmy bit her tongue. Why did everyone assume that getting married was the only thing she could or might want to achieve?

The tour continued. Auntie Beattie duly admired the dusty-pink spun-glass tulips from Woolworth's, the rearing cast-iron horses on the mantel, the beautiful carpet with clusters of acorns, and the luxurious leather suite in palest green with forest green velvet cushions. They had tea in Dibbs's with Beryl and Eddie and got the trolleybus to the beach.

'If you knew how I've dreamed of one day walking in the sand,' Elizabeth Whately murmured to Emmy as they went along the prom. 'But this is the next best thing.'

They saw Auntie Beattie off on the six o'clock train.

'Now let's go to the pictures!'

'Are you sure?' Emmy thought she looked tired. Her cheeks were shiny from being in the sun, her eyes unnaturally bright. In the queue outside the picture-house, she was full of excited chatter about Beryl's plans for the shop.

'She's got your pop's ambition all right. Furniture next, she reckons, everyone needs furniture. And jewellery. When I think how we started out on a shoestring! What did he always say? We go up or we go—Oh!' She clutched Emmy's arm. 'Oh, Emmy!'

'What is it?' cried Emmy.

'The world's going round . . . ' Elizabeth Whately closed her eyes tightly, as if to shut out some frightful thing. How tiny she was in Emmy's arms, like a kitten, all bones. 'Oh!' She opened her eyes again, and blinked several times. 'That's better! Don't look so frightened, Em. All back to normal!'

'Hadn't we better go home?'

'Nonsense! It's just my age.'

A voice whispered then in Emmy's ear: something is wrong. But it was a voice she didn't want to hear.

The grass grew fast and was forever in need of cutting. Emmy dreamed that it rose above the roof until only a chimney-pot stuck out, like the tip of a church spire from a flooded valley. Things were out of control in some way that she didn't understand.

Coming home one night, she saw an old woman, hobbling in at their front gate. The woman smiled at her and waved. Who's that? wondered Emmy, smiling back out of politeness.

It was her mother.

The doctor made an appointment for Elizabeth Whately at the hospital.

'It's these silly dizzy spells,' Mother apologized. 'You know how they like to be sure. I'll go just to please them. On my own. No need for any fuss.'

A week later, Emmy walked in from work and found Gus waiting for her.

'She's gone to our Beryl's. We're all going.' He couldn't say any more. He handed her a letter which said it for him.

Something had burst in the back of Elizabeth Whately's head and was bleeding into the brain. There was nothing the doctors could do. The weakness and dizziness would get worse. There was a place for her in the free hospital if she wanted it. Where the old people went to die.

'She's not going to die, though, is she?' said Gus. 'They'll fix her up, won't they? Like they did before?'

Emmy thought he was going to cry. She wanted him to. She wanted not to have to be strong, to be able to weep with somebody, to comfort and be comforted.

'I'm going out,' he said. 'I'll see you.'

Beryl made up a bed for Elizabeth Whately in her old upstairs parlour, and set a chair in the window so that she could look out into the street. The new house was rented to strangers. The furniture went into the shop to be sold second-hand.

Winter came. Spring came. Elizabeth Whately sat in her window for a little while each day. Then a little each week. Then not at all. But Emmy could never break herself of the habit of looking up to check as she hurried home from work.

That summer, she seemed never to stop running. She rushed out in the morning, rushed home at dinner-time, rushed back to work, rushed back home again. Sometimes she paused for a moment on the Coast Road to watch the lorry perched at the top of the slag heap teeter and tip out its load of boiling spoil—a gush of brightness against the fading sky—but only ever for a moment. And on Sundays she went to the beach and ran and swam and played and laughed as if her life depended on it. Golden laughter, edged with guilt. *In an upstairs room my mother is dying. In a small upstairs room, my mother is disappearing and dying . . .*

Gus couldn't stand it. He came in one day and told them, 'I've joined the RAF. Ground staff. I leave in two days.' He went upstairs to tell his mother. 'We had to do an exam. I came top. Ninety-seven per cent.' She smiled at him with eyes full of tenderness. He held the pad steady for her to write her answer. When he read out what she had written, his voice shook.

'You deserve this. They never gave you a chance at school. Take care. I love you.'

In the autumn Emmy gave in her notice at the grocer's. Elizabeth Whately was never going to leave the upstairs room, never walk on the beach. It was the time of their greatest prosperity and she was starving to death. No longer able to speak or to swallow, she had to feed herself with a rubber tube the way they force-fed prisoners in jail. There came a time when she had not the strength to do it for herself. A nurse came then to help her. The people in the street stifled their footsteps when they passed by the house where they knew that Death was waiting, silent and patient, an unacknowledged guest.

The doctor came. He gave her morphine to help her sleep. It was Emmy's turn to sit with her. She held the small hand, frail as a wafer, and still smelling of bleach, or so Emmy persuaded herself, and listened to her breathing. They had opened a window to let out the sick-room stuffiness. On the chill night air, she heard a gentle tenor voice:

'I'll take you home again, Kathleen,
Across the ocean wild and wide . . . '

It might have been a man at an open window, shaving, to save time in the morning. Or a gramophone record perhaps. Or perhaps the familiar words came from inside her own head, for it had always been one of Father's favourite songs . . .

'The roses all have left your cheeks
I watched them fade away and die . . . '

Her mother's rosy cheeks. Not a sign of health at all, but of dangerously high blood-pressure. Brought on by what? She had never weighed more than six stone.

'To where the fields are fresh and green . . .
I will take you home again—Kathleen!'

132

Silence.

The sound of a distant train leaving.

Then a more complete silence.

'The doctor said she would go tonight,' said Beryl.

'How did he know?'

'Maybe he took pity on her.' Beryl drew up the sheet like a calm, pale wave to cover the weary, lovely face.

'Poor Gus. How will we tell him? He loved his mother so.'

All the aunts who were still living came to the funeral. Auntie Beattie, whose puddings were so firm you could cut them like cake. Auntie Franny, who prayed in the bathroom. Aunties Peggy and Annie and Minnie. As unmarried girls, each of the aunts would have prepared a 'hope chest', into which she put lace for her bridal veil, sheets for her wedding-bed, layettes for the babies to come. The years had passed, the sheets had got mended sides to middle, the clothes had got grown out of and passed down. And as the years passed, wondered Emmy, did each of the aunts fill up another, secret chest, full of lost hopes, dead babies, griefs that had to be hidden from the men in case they went away? A grief chest?

How strong and upright they all were, and all so much older than Elizabeth Whately, 'the runt of the litter,' as she had called herself. Remembering, Emmy felt her heart swell with anguish. She could feel Auntie Beattie looking, wondering why she wasn't weeping, but the habit of holding back was so ingrained that if she had let out her feelings, they would have seemed manufactured, artificial. Didn't they know that if she let herself start, she would never stop, until the church and all the mourners and the coffin and the flowers and the organ-player were carried out of the town on a tide of grief, out as far as the mermaids under the North Sea, the cold, sensible mermaids who never yearned to walk on the dry land?

After the funeral, Gus had to get back to his regiment.

'He looks a fine young man in his uniform,' said Aunt Beattie. 'He'll turn out well, if he's spared. So there's only you left, Emmeline. Have you decided what you're going to do? You know what I mean. Is there anyone in the offing?'

Emmy reddened.

'Nobody,' she said.

'Well, you can't live with your sister all your life. You know what they say, three's a crowd. When war comes, you won't be able to pick and choose.' They talk about it coming as if it were a season, thought Emmy. An inevitability, like winter. Make sure you've got yourself a husband in case there's a shortage. As if a man were a sack of coal.

22

'So that's why you came to London?'

'Partly. I felt so lost. Abandoned. They didn't just go away, Milly, they *died*. Of overwork and anxiety and grief and disappointment and living too long on a knife's edge. It seemed as if every time things were going right, something had to come and sweep it all away.' Gran tucked a wisp of hair behind my ear. I still had my head on her knee, the safest place in the world. 'Besides—they were offering six weeks' guaranteed work at two pounds a week!' She chuckled. 'Everyone thought I was mad with a war coming, but I was optimistic then, even in the midst of that terrible sorrow. I had to be. Up or under. I'm not now. If I don't find her face here, I don't think I could bear it . . . Can you forgive me?'

'It's you who should be forgiving *me.*'

'Don't be daft.'

'I brought you here under false pretences.' I couldn't go on lying, not even me, the Champion Liar, not now. 'Mum and Dad aren't getting back together, ever, and I couldn't face it. Dad's going to marry Sherrylynne. They're having a baby.' Gran stopped stroking my hair. 'They told us on Friday night . . . Gran . . . ?'

'Where's Joanna? You didn't leave her on her own?'

'We had a row.' How pathetic it sounded. 'I said some stuff . . . '

'What stuff?'

'You know . . . ' I mumbled it into her knees. ' . . . like it was all her fault . . . driving Dad away.' Gran reached

135

for the phone. 'You *mustn't call her*!' I sat up fast. 'I promised I wouldn't tell!'

'Why not?'

'She thinks you'll blame her too.'

'Oh, *Milly* . . . '

'I wanted to hide it from you,' I babbled. 'I wanted to protect you. That's what this weekend was all about.'

'Oh, come on! You wanted to protect yourself, and you used my mother as an excuse! So when do you think Joanna will pluck up the nerve to tell me?' I had hurt her badly, I could tell. 'When she has absolutely no choice, I suppose.'

'It's not like that.'

'And what *is* it like? No, don't tell me, I'm sure I couldn't possibly understand. Have you done your packing? We'll make a start first thing.'

'But—'

'I have to be with her, Milly. Even if she *never* tells me. Some things you can't tear up. She's my daughter. She needs me.'

'She doesn't need anybody,' I muttered. 'She's got her coven.'

'*Milly!* You know she'd come running if *you* were in trouble.'

'She won't ever have to. You don't have to worry about *me*, any of you. I'll *always* shut my lips and shout sugar.'

'D'you think I wouldn't have loved to have somebody to listen? You should let your mother see you like this sometimes. It's a terrible burden, she told me once, having a perfect daughter.'

'I'm *not* perfect!' If only she knew! 'I'm not even adequate!'

We went to bed early, and lay listening to each other's

breathing. I wanted so badly to cry, but I didn't dare to with Gran in the next bed. Even the en-suite bathroom was too risky.

Some time after midnight, she whispered across the divide, 'Milly? Are you awake?'

I'll swear she didn't want me to hear. Maybe that's why I didn't answer. Maybe if I had, she wouldn't have said what she did. I don't know. It's a lousy excuse anyway.

'I'm frightened, Milly. I feel like an old ghost that nobody remembers any more. Coming here has made me realize what I am. I never felt old before. Not like this.'

I wanted to say something, but I couldn't. I had become an eavesdropper.

'I don't know if I can drive all that way back, Milly. I hurt. I'm so scared, Milly. I'm so scared.'

She started to cry in a furtive, desperate way. I wanted to get out of bed and jump in with her and hug her tired, tiny body and rock her like a baby. But I'd left it too late.

And I didn't have any answers.

'Of course I'm all right!' she snapped. 'Why shouldn't I be?'

'Gran, you haven't been well since we arrived.'

'That's just the food, enough to make anyone sick.'

'Couldn't you see a doctor or somebody before we go? Just to check you out?'

'We are not bringing doctors into this. Understand?' Gran threw her curlers into her vanity bag. 'If you want to get us both back in one piece—' She snapped a couple of pills out of their foil case and dry-swallowed, squinting with disgust '—you'll just get yourself tidied up now and stop arguing.'

137

I couldn't bear it. Watching her hobbling about, looking about a hundred and twenty, too scared to call a doctor. Shutting her lips and shouting sugar.

'And you are never, *ever* to tell Joanna about this, do you understand? If there's one thing I learned at a very early age, it's to keep your disasters to yourself. We're leaving in five minutes. Got it?' She went into the bathroom. I waited until I heard the water running, then I picked up the phone and dialled very fast.

Come on, come on, come on, come on!

'Yo!' said Mum's voice. 'I'm not here! But just hang on, and this wonderful device will transfer you to the mobile—'

'Five minutes!' called Gran.

'Hello?' It was Mum's real voice. 'Hello! Anybody there?'

I heard the bathroom door opening.

'Milly? Is that you? Milly?'

Help me, I mouthed, and set the receiver down again with a feeling of utter hopelessness.

'Careful, Gran! The cyclist!'

'I *saw* it. They should stick to the psychopaths, getting under everybody's feet. Shouldn't we be on the motorway by now?'

'This is a quieter route. You haven't got your seat belt on!'

'It's too tight.'

'Gran, it's the *law*.'

'It's cutting off the blood in my fingers. I can't feel the wheel this side for pins and needles.'

'If you haven't got it on, how—*Gran, look out!*' I saw the lorry, the lorry driver's jaw dropping open below his sunglasses, I pretty well saw the teeth-marks in his chewing-gum, and I grabbed the wheel, actually grabbed it, just like they do on TV, and swerved us out of his path. 'Omigod, Gran, didn't you *see* him? Gran?'

She was clinging to the wheel, her face white and wet.

'Straighten up, Gran.'

'I can't feel my fingers, Emmy.'

'OK, OK, pull over. You've had a shock. Pull over.'

'I don't know what to do with my—'

'*Brake*, Gran. Get your foot off the accel—Put your foot on the brake, Gran! The one in the middle! GRAN!'

We slowed down and started weaving towards the side of the road. I grabbed the handbrake and finished the job with a jolt. Sweat jumped out of me from every pore.

'Got get out . . . ' Gran was trying to open her door.

'Not that side, Gran.' The traffic was whizzing past fast enough to singe the hairs off her arms. 'Shuffle across.' I found her handbag. 'Which pills d'you need?'

'The sea . . . ' She pushed past me. 'Got to find the sea . . . ' She tottered a few steps over the grass, folded up and sat down in a sudden heap like a toddler.

'Which pills, Gran?'

She fell backwards and lay still.

'GRAN!'

I knelt beside her. Her lips were a horrible blue round the edges, as if she'd been drinking ink. 'Oh, God. Oh, Gran. Be all right, Gran, *please*!' I grabbled round in her bag and found her compact. I couldn't open it. My fingers were like sponge fingers. I could have chewed them off and spat them out and not felt a thing. 'Come on, come *on*! Get a *grip*.' I got the compact open and held the mirror to her mouth.

Nothing.

'What do I *do*? Tell me what to do, Gran!'

Gran wasn't about to tell me anything.

And then, out of the blue, Miss Anderson's first aid

classes kicked in. I was suddenly utterly calm in a way
I've never been before or since.

'OK, OK. We can do this, Gran.' I lifted off her glasses,
making sure I didn't catch them on her ears. I tilted her
head back and checked the airways. I pinched her nostrils
together. I took a breath. I breathed it into her. Carefully,
carefully. Like it says in the Highway Code, gently, for a
child. After two seconds, I stopped blowing and checked
that her chest was falling. Then I did it again.

After my fourth go, the sweat was pouring into my
eyes. But Gran still wasn't breathing for herself.

Someone was humming. I looked up, and saw Emmy,
sitting just a few yards away, gazing out across the dual
carriageway. It was as if Gran's spirit had jumped right
out of her body. She was aged about seven, and she was
wearing her second-hand white dress for the journey to
White Burn Sands. She was on her way home.

I wanted to hammer on Gran's chest like a streetful of
angry men, like a team of TV surgeons in a hospital soap.
But I forced myself to concentrate, to keep the rhythm, to
push my breath, my spirit, into her, over and over again.

The humming stopped. I looked up in agony.

'Emmy—no! *Please!*'

Emmy turned her head slowly and stared in my
direction. She had a puzzled expression, as if she were
trying to see through a gauze. Then she smiled, she smiled
right at me, and began to disappear like breath from a
window-pane, and I felt Gran's chest rising under my
fingers, and I heard a great beating of wings, like the
blades of a helicopter swishing overhead, and as Gran
began breathing, harshly at first, with a sound like a car
struggling over a snowy road, then with greater
confidence, the helicopter spoke to me:

'Milly! Milly! Thank God!' And was Dad.

'You're safe now, Milly!' And was Mum.

23

'You can go in and see her now,' said the nurse.
Mum held my right hand. Dad held my left.
Like they used to when I was little, and they could swing me between them with my feet right off the ground. We went in together.

Gran lay on the bed, looking like a teddy-bear behind the plastic snout of her oxygen mask, her frost-frizzled hair straggling over the pillow, and plastic bottles of her vital essences hooked up all around her, attached to her by tubes. As if they'd taken out her blood and her tears and her hormones and her pheromones and her moods and her memories, and clipped them all up on a rail for easy access.

I could feel Mum's trembling all the way up my right arm and into my teeth. She was trying not to cry. That's *her* mum, I thought. If *I'm* terrified, how much worse must it be for *her*? Suddenly I wanted to be able to tell her things, silly things, important things, it didn't matter, just so she'd feel she was the sort of mum you could tell things to.

I felt Dad's hand squeezing mine on the other side.

'Let's give them a moment,' he murmured. I untangled my fingers from Mum's. It felt like the worst kind of desertion. And then Gran opened her eyes and looked at Mum, and smiled. The kind of smile you'd give your whole life to have smiled at you.

'*There* you are!' she said.

We tiptoed away.

141

'Is she going to be all right?' Sherrylynne put down her magazine. She looked genuinely anxious, and a bit embarrassed about asking. She had a zit coming on her chin, the only bump she had yet, as far as I could see. She was way too skinny. I hoped she wasn't starving my little brother or sister just to look trendy. I'd have to take her in hand.

'Right as rain,' said the nurse. 'Thanks to this one here.' She beamed at me. If she'd known the facts, she'd have thrown me over her shoulder, carried me off to the sluice-room and flushed me down the pan.

There was a bit of an awkward pause.

'I'll get us some coffees, shall I?' said Dad. 'Will you be—?' He didn't look too happy about leaving us alone.

'We'll be fine.' I couldn't see why it had ever been a problem. It just didn't seem to matter any more.

He hurried off.

Mum came out.

'Is she OK?'

'She will be. Oh, Milly. How could you do something so stupid? So irresponsible? Junketing round the country with my mother—*my mother*! She's never even driven on a motorway—' Sherrylynne did a passable imitation of a whippet chasing a sausage on a bit of elastic, and vanished into the Ladies. 'Honestly, Milly, I could kill you!' I was glad she was letting me have it. It was time somebody did. 'You're supposed to have this great bond with your gran, and when it comes down to it, you were just using her as an excuse to run away! You could have killed her! You could both have been—' She burst into tears, and grabbed hold of me, and held on to me like she thought I was about to be whizzed out through the ceiling on a wire by the SAS. 'Don't you ever, *ever* frighten us like that again! You could have been killed. You could both . . . I daren't even think about it . . . '

It was a lovely feeling, Mum crying on my shoulder. Because I was crying on hers at the same time, and that was a first. I hadn't even cried openly when the paramedics arrived and I saw them zipping Gran up into a bag.

We drew apart and got fresh Kleenexes and honked at each other like a couple of seals.

'You know I don't really want to shout at you.'

'Yes you do. You love it.'

'Not when it's something that really matters.'

'How did you know where we were?' I hadn't even thought to ask before. You just expect your mum and dad to be there in a crisis.

'I dialled 1471. I knew it was you. It was engaged for ages. By the time I got through, you'd checked out.'

'But how did you get to us so fast?'

'We were already there! In a hotel on the other side of town! Your dad realized you'd gone off somewhere. He waited around for you most of Sunday, then he let himself in with his key. Mum gave us both one. We thought it was only sensible, what with her angina getting so much worse this last year . . . '

'Why didn't anybody *tell* me?'

'You had too much on your plate, Milly. You were being so desperately brave, shutting your lips and shouting sugar . . . ' Mum laughed. 'I haven't used that expression in years! Your gran used to say it to me—'

'You never said it to *me*.'

'I never needed to! Anyway, you'd left the map out on the table—and that's not like you—with the routes marked. So he called me, and we decided to go after you. When we got through to your hotel, the manageress said she thought Gran was looking shaky, and she'd left her angina spray behind, so we knew we had to act fast.'

I knew then that I'd always have them. Both of them.

On different terms from before, maybe, but, like Gran said, some things you can't tear up. And I took Mum's face, just as it was right then, and put it in my heart, to hold there for ever.

'Hello, Milly. I've had *such* a lovely sleep!'

'Have you, Gran?' I sat down beside her and took her hand in mine. It was so thin and cold, with tubes sticking out of the veins in the back of it, making bruises in the puckered skin.

'And the loveliest dream . . . '

'Tell me about it.'

'I was a little girl again, in my best white dress . . . It was the day we first came to White Burn Sands. I was looking at the sea and thinking, this is where I want to stay for ever and ever, I don't want it ever to change . . . '

'That's nice, Gran.'

'But it *did* change, Milly . . . Into a beautiful green field. And I saw an old, old lady lying there, and I thought, nothing will ever change for her any more . . . and I didn't know whether to be happy or sad. Then I saw this pretty young girl kneeling beside her, kissing her. And d'you know who it was? It was *you*, Milly! And I knew then who the old lady was, and I thought: if nothing changes, this will never happen to me, and it was a part of my life that I didn't want to miss. And then I woke up. I've been quite poorly, haven't I?'

'It was my fault, Gran. Dragging you all that way.'

'Darling, I *wanted* to go.'

'But you never found Elizabeth Whately's face.'

'I did! I did! And it's where I can never lose it again!'

'Where?'

'Look in my handbag!'

'How can—?'

'Just open it up. There's something I want you to have.'

'What is it?'

'You just keep looking until you find it. And while you're looking, there's a postscript to my story that I never told you. You think it all ended so sadly, but it's like *you* said . . . happiness and sorrow are all mixed up together . . .'

*   *   *

She put down her suitcase and went into the upstairs parlour. She wanted to touch something that Elizabeth Whately had touched. The bed had been taken away. There was no wardrobe full of friendly ghosts, of hats wrinkled and warped into the shape of a beloved head. An empty chair stood in the window. On the floor next to it was her mother's old handbag, wizened and misshapen, flat-bottomed like a muffin from being dumped whenever and wherever she sat down.

Emmy parted the curtains and gazed out into the street. Will I look back one day, she wondered, and see it all golden and perfect, as you're supposed to remember your childhood, sealed up forever in the sunshine of a summer afternoon? Or will I remember only the shadows?

She sat down in the chair and lifted the bag on to her knee. She ran her fingers over the handle, worn thin where Mother used to loop it over her arm. On the sleeve of Mother's old coat there was a correspondingly shiny patch . . .

She undid the clasp, and the smell of English Lavender from a bruised handkerchief rose to meet her nostrils. She drew out the old leather purse, creased and worn as a beloved face.

Inside was a single sixpence.

'Remember?' Beryl had come softly up behind her. 'As long as I have a sixpence in my purse . . .'

It might have been newly minted. The milled edge was rough under her thumbnail. But the face was King Edward VII's, and the date was 1908, the year Mother and Father had been wed.

And at last she was able to cry.

The train jolted, and she sat down, feeling as if everyone were staring at her. Fighting the urge to fix the angle of her hat or get out her powder-puff, she made herself look out of the window. All along the beach they were putting up barbed-wire, as if to keep the sea from coming into town. War. Everything would change soon for everybody.

The train went into a tunnel and all the lights came on, and a face stared in through the blackened window, a face with huge, hungry eyes, that might have been those of a bewildered six year old. Then they rushed out of the darkness again and the light was so bright and glorious and the hedges so green and the sky so blue, it was as if she had emerged from deep water into a brilliant new day. She shivered with anticipation, as if shaking waterdrops out of her hair. Seeing her smile, the other people in the carriage all smiled too. I'm a pretty young girl, she thought with delight, seeing herself with their eyes. I've taken the plunge and everything is just beginning.

*   *   *

'Have you found it?' said Gran.

I had. The lucky sixpence. Thin as a sucked sweet. Fragile as a baby's fingerprint. I was almost afraid of it.

'It's yours now. You're the keeper of the memories now.'

I squeezed her hand. She was going to be all right. We were all going to be all right. Different, not like we'd

146

planned, but all right. I was getting over it, in spite of myself. That's what you do. You honour the past, but you don't have to be its slave. You go up, not under.

'And Elizabeth Whately's face?'

'You really haven't guessed yet?' She smiled. 'Surely you must know that your mother's middle name is Elizabeth?'

There you are!

Of course. I knew now why I had never felt any burning need to fit a face into the space where Elizabeth Whately's should have been. It was a space for a mother's face. And that's what I'd put there already, without even realizing . . .

There's a postscript to my story too. A week after we got home, an envelope plopped through the letter box. It was the photos. There was no note: I wondered uneasily if he'd try and get in touch. I owed him the money, after all.

'Was he a . . . *nice* . . . boy?' asked Mum, trying to sound casual and rubbing at the crease between her eyebrows.

'Don't worry. The Worst didn't happen.'

'I wasn't asking.'

'It was a near thing, though.' That was as generous as I was prepared to be. It was a big stride for me, believe me.

'Is this him?' Mum passed me the shot of the arcade featuring Elizabeth Whately's window. Her empty window.

'Where?'

'The reflection.'

I looked again, and saw myself, in the downstairs pane, aiming the camera. A little to my left, half turned away and lighting a rollie, was Dominic. My initial reaction was a rush of shamed disgust, like the spurt of lager that washes over the top of the tin when you snap the ring. But it passed almost at once. Poor Dominic. Rejected by his mum, by his kid's mum, by pretty well everyone. He had shown me more charity than I deserved. I wished somebody had cared enough about him to have done something about his teeth.

'I'm ready now!' Gran had been hunting for her specs. 'Can I see?' I handed her the snap.

'It's just an empty window. Are you very disappointed?'

'Disappointed?' Her face was shining. 'Don't you see, Milly? It doesn't *matter* that she's not there—I can still see her! Sitting there, looking down into the street, in her old blouse with the leg-of-mutton sleeves that she never threw away . . . the image of your mother . . . My father asked her once what it was she saw from the window that was so fascinating. You know what she said? The *future*. And here it is! Here *you* are! A ghost of the future!'

Funny, isn't it? You can try so hard to spoil things for yourself. And the stuff you do almost without thinking puts it all back on course again.

'Who's this?' Mum held up a photo of a little boy. He was aged about ten with bright red hair and a shy grin. 'It's from a different batch.' She turned it over. '*Jimmy. August 1999*. Who's Jimmy?'

I looked at it for a long moment.

'That's a face somebody thought he'd run away from for good . . . But it looks like they caught up with each other in the end.'

I was glad he'd let me know.

It meant we'd all been forgiven.

Other books by Pamela Scobie

The School That Went On Strike
ISBN 0 19 275051 8

On 1 April 1914 the Headmistress and Assistant Master of
Burston Council School were sacked by the Managers. As they
were handing over to the Authorities, they heard the sound of
children marching and singing. The schoolchildren—66 out of
72—had gone on strike.

This is the fictionalized story of that strike. The story of how
the Headmistress, Annie Higdon, fought the Managers for
decent conditions in the school, which was damp, cold, and
unhygienic; and of how her husband Tom campaigned to
create fair and just living conditions for the farm labourers. For
all this they were told to leave.

But the children of the school believed in the goodness of their
teachers and came out on strike. Led by a 13-year-old girl, they
marched around the village with placards and refused to go
back to school. The Authorities put pressure on their parents
and imposed severe fines. But the strike continued. It turned
out to be the longest strike in British history and lasted for 25
years.

Based on true events, this is an enthralling novel about a group
of children who came together to fight for goodness and
justice—it's the story of the school that went on strike.

Shortlisted for the Whitbread Children's Award.

'This is a powerful story, powerfully written.'
The School Librarian

'The tingle factor is unmistakably there.'
Daily Mail

Children of the Wheel

ISBN 0 19 271662 X

'They're coming!' shouted Axl. 'Hide the baby, quick!'
'We could make a run for it . . . '
'We'd never make it. There are soldiers at both ends of the streets with
nets. Come on!'

The City's in trouble, gripped by famine, poisoned by
pollution. So what do you do? Get rid of the garbage. Get rid of
the kids, especially the Damaged ones, or those who don't
conform. Round them up, shove them out, let them fend for
themselves. Till you need them again. Then drag them
screaming back into what *you* call civilization . . .

But what if they've *learned* something out there in the
Wilderness? What if they've found out a secret bigger than any
of you, bigger than your City, bigger than your whole world?

That's what Cyndra did. And when they wanted her back, they
got more than they bargained for . . .

'an epic read'
     CLAI

150